"There'll Be No Parting As Friends.

You can't have it both ways."

Holly touched her cheek with surprisingly cold fingers as she thought about how she must look. His last words stung. This time she was sure he would drop his hands and go; she wanted him to go. Which was why, when he bent his head to kiss her, she gasped.

"What are you doing?"

"Giving you the kiss you expected a while ago, driving you wild with passion, making you helpless with desire. To be perfectly honest, I'm going to do it again."

Holly Bancroft stood on tiptoes in Drew Branigan's house and let herself be kissed senseless. He expects me to protest, to scream and carry on, she thought. Wild with passion? Maybe. Helpless with desire? Never! She would never be helpless.

Dear Reader,

Welcome to Silhouette! Our goal is to give you hours of unbeatable reading pleasure, and we hope you'll enjoy each month's six new Silhouette Desires. These sensual, provocative love stories are both believable and compelling—sometimes they're poignant, sometimes humorous, but always enjoyable.

Indulge yourself. Experience all the passion and excitement of falling in love along with our heroine as she meets the irresistible man of her dreams and together they overcome all obstacles in the path to a happy ending.

If this is your first Desire, I hope it'll be the first of many. If you're already a Silhouette Desire reader, thanks for your support! Look for some of your favorite authors in the coming months: Stephanie James, Diana Palmer, Dixie Browning, Ann Major and Doreen Owens Malek, to name just a few.

Happy reading!

Isabel Swift
Senior Editor

SDRL-7/85

LESLIE DAVIS GUCCIONE
Bittersweet Harvest

Silhouette Desire

Published by Silhouette Books New York

America's Publisher of Contemporary Romance

I got by with a little help from my friends...

John and Barbara Cook who hunt and inspired the opening scene; Paige and Sherb Carter who know about romance among the bogs; Suzanne R. Davis, R.N., and the men of the Duxbury Fire Department who answered my questions; William J. Harriman, Deputy Chief and cranberry grower, whose expertise helped this ring true; and especially Edward S. Davis II, who escorted me to *Carmen* at the Old Met, my first opera.

SILHOUETTE BOOKS
300 East 42nd St., New York, N.Y. 10017

Books by Leslie Davis Guccione

Silhouette Desire

Before the Wind #279
Bittersweet Harvest #311

LESLIE DAVIS GUCCIONE

lives with her husband and three children in a state of semi-chaos in a historic sea captains' district south of Boston. When she's not at her typewriter she's actively researching everything from sailboats to cranberry bogs. What free time she has is spent sailing and restoring her circa 1827 Cape Cod cottage. Her ideas for her books are based on the world around her. As she states, "Romance is right under your nose." She has also written under the name Leslie Davis.

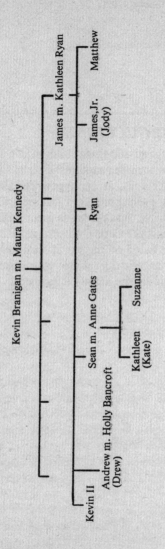

BRANIGAN FAMILY TREE

Kevin Branigan m. Maura Kennedy

Sean m. Anne Gates

Kathleen (Kate)

Suzanne

Ryan

James m. Kathleen Ryan

James, Jr. (Jody)

Matthew

Andrew m. Holly Bancroft (Drew)

Kevin II

One

The volume at which Holly Bancroft was playing her uncle's opera records should have driven everything else from her mind. Placido Domingo's soulful tenor filled the cozy Greek Revival farmhouse to bursting; Pagliacci's heart was breaking but still Holly thought about the Branigan brothers.

Putting Bittersweet Bogs up for sale without notifying them first had been a major tactical error, a purely emotional act to sever the ties to her distant, dishonest uncle. Peter Bancroft had spent nineteen years hovering over the six country orphans next door, and now every last one of the Branigans had let her know in no uncertain terms that she had a fight on her hands.

Holly sat alone in the parlor of her inherited house, her heart thumping at the memory of their wrath. *Kevin, Andrew, Sean, Ryan, James and Matthew* she had memorized before their impromptu meeting the evening before, concentrating on Kevin and Drew, as Andrew was called, the major partners of Branigan Cranberries. Holly was fair, slight and, at just under five and a half feet, prided herself on not being as vulnerable as she appeared. In fact, in the six years she had been teaching English to Philadelphia's Italian immigrants, there had never been an episode she hadn't been able to resolve with humor, kindness and professionalism.

None of it had worked on the Branigans. She realized now—almost too late—that she needed more strategy, an iron will and a masculine perspective if she were going to get anywhere with them. They had all offered opinions, keeping her off balance throughout the entire confrontation. It wouldn't happen again.

Her hand trembled in frustration even now as she tried to apply polish to the last of her toes. Her conflict with Peter Bancroft's nearest neighbors was a professional one. She asked only that they let her do what she had every legal right to do, and get herself out of the sand hills and cranberry bogs of Millbrook, Massachusetts.

She finished the pedicure and looked beyond her feet to the fire on the hearth. In front of her, seasoned wood burned furiously, crackling and spitting, throwing warmth into the room. Holly wiggled her toes, admiring the contrast of Crimson Blush and the white cotton balls separating her toes. Domingo's voice broke into a tirade and she raised her glass of kir. "You said it," she toasted.

Her Uncle Peter Bancroft a man she had loved, then been taught to hate, then been forced to forget, had become more baffling in death than he had ever been in her troubled life. He had left Holly his entire estate, which included receiving monthly payments on a loan from the thriving business next door. She sipped her drink of kir, a wine aperitif, and mulled over the situation until she was interrupted by a sharp rap on her uncle's front door.

It came again, hard, impatient, as if she hadn't heard it the first time. Unconsciously she pressed her free hand over her hammering heart. From the couch she could make out a dark form on the farmer's unlit porch. She wasn't expecting anyone; she didn't know anyone except the Boston realtor and her six neighbors who had made it clear they intended to deal with her as little as possible.

Holly got up, duck-walking on her heels, trying to work on a calm expression. It wasn't easy. From fifteen feet she could see that the figure was tall, shadowed; a male. From ten feet she could make out through the side panes the splotched pattern of a camouflage jacket. She sucked in a deep breath.

She wasn't about to open her door to anyone she didn't know, not at home in Philadelphia and certainly not here in the wilds of Millbrook. The alien environment increased her hesitancy tenfold.

When nothing separated them but the panes of glass, the figure turned to face her, gave her a smile that would have melted steel and waited. Holly's hand went back over her breast. She recognized the face although the smile was new. But she wasn't entirely sure which Branigan was grinning at her. Her pulse rate doubled as she opened the door to six feet of duck hunter.

"You weren't expecting me," he said, looking from her padded toes to the direction of the music.

"You can hardly blame me," she replied, sure that the incredibly green eyes had belonged to the identical twins.

He stepped over the threshold into the foyer as she looked at the hunting jacket, chest-high waders and wooden duck call hanging around his neck from a raw-hide strip. He mumbled *Pagliacci* as he pulled his watch cap from his head with his left hand. No wedding band, she thought. Sean was the married twin.

"I can't stay," he said, the cold October air clinging to him.

"I wasn't going to ask you to, Drew." There!

His grin stayed in place. "Very good. 'Bout the only way to tell us apart is Sean's wedding band. Astute observation." He seemed delighted that she looked discomforted. Before closing the door he stooped to pick up something on the porch floor. Back inside he thrust a dead duck within inches of Holly's nose. She gave a cry and, hand again to heart, backed in the direction of the stereo.

"Peace offering. I thought after last night one of us should come over." Drew started past her in the direction of the kitchen.

"After last night I hardly care whether I ever see any of you again," she called, hobbling after him, yanking cotton pads as she went through the parlor, dining room and up to the kitchen sink. "Besides, assuming you just shot that poor, defenseless thing, you should know that I loathe hunting. I haven't the faintest idea how to undress it and I don't want it!"

A smile lit his face, and warmed the eyes that had stared so coldly the night before. "You don't *un*dress a duck, you dress it. Watch me while I breast it. You owe it to yourself to give it a try." He glanced at her feet. "Athlete's foot?"

She sniffed. "Don't be ridiculous, I just polished my toenails. You're changing the subject."

He shrugged. "Do you always go barefoot when frost is threatened?"

Holly pulled the wastebasket from beneath the sink and set it between them. She dropped in the cotton, and he dropped in some feathers. "That's really none of your business, Drew."

"True, but not having any sisters, I find these female rituals absolutely fascinating when I come across them." Andrew Branigan, all six feet of him, looked as though he might come across female rituals with great frequency, a lack of sisters notwithstanding. Holly stole a glance at the planes of his face as his lips puckered and he gently blew feathers from the duck. Downy drifts scattered across the Formica.

She had to clear her throat. "You're making a terrible mess."

His smile seemed permanent. "Worth it. Trust me and I give you my word, I'll clean up every last feather."

"I said I didn't want it."

He pulled out a hunting knife, reacting to her gasp with arched eyebrows. "Holly—is that some sort of a nickname or were you born on Christmas?"

"December twenty-third, not that—"

"It's any of my business. Sweet name for such an obstinate woman. Everything about you is my business, *our* business...now. Look, the duck was an excuse to come over and tell you we might have been a little rough on you last night." He gestured toward the bird. "You can do what you want with these, but I'd advise giving it a try. Sautée—"

"I don't want your advice or your peace offering! What I deserve is an apology from all of you."

Drew cut the fillets from the bone and then placed them on the counter. He began to collect the carcass and feathers. "Don't misunderstand. No one's going to apologize for what we hold sacred and no one's going to stand by while you destroy this land."

"It isn't *this* land, it's my property now." She braced herself for a flash of Irish temper.

Drew turned his clear green gaze on her, high color across his cheeks. "You're moving too fast. You don't give a damn about Millbrook because you haven't given yourself a chance to. You don't care—"

"You should have taken that up with my uncle since you were like sons to him." Holly bowed her head, plucking a feather from her woolen pants. "The invitation to know Millbrook, to care about it, was never extended to me. He nearly ruined my father, something I'm sure he never mentioned. This business was bought with money he took from Dad and his business."

"And selling it will let you pay back a twenty-year-old debt?"

"My parents are both gone. My reasons are my own." Her color was beginning to match his. She'd said more than she had meant to, to a member of the one family who stood between her and financial independence; the one family who had always stood in the way. Holly stiffened, prepared for Drew's backlash. When it didn't come, she raised her head. He was looking at her as if he had absorbed not only her words, but the pain, as well.

"I resent the fact that the six Branigan brothers are so determined to make mincemeat out of me."

He pulled a paper towel from over the sink and wiped the counter. "Look at it from our point of view. Six orphans trying to make their way in the world, struggling to keep the family afloat, knee-deep in debt to modernize our equipment..."

"My Aunt Fannie."

Drew smiled. "You don't have an Aunt Fannie."

Holly put her hands on her hip. "You debt is only ankle deep—Branigan Cranberries is thriving. And since you borrowed from Peter and you all think he was such a saint, why did he will the loan to me, Drew? Why didn't your beloved mentor at least cancel the debt? Why didn't he leave you his six acres of bogs for that matter? It wouldn't have taken much to slice off the far corner of this property."

His reply was as clipped as her accusation. "He assumed that his beneficiary would have the same ideals and principles as he did, maybe that she'd come to Millbrook and carry on the tradition."

"You're as crazy as he was if you honestly believe that. Peter Bancroft turned his back on me when I was ten. We wouldn't have recognized each other if we met. The man had no interest in my goals, ideals or principles." She jammed a tortoise-shell comb into her tangle of hair for lack of anything better to do with her hands. The house was still, the strains of *Pagliacci* suddenly over. "Peter Bancroft should have made stipulations in his will. What I'm doing makes sound business sense. I'm looking out for myself, which is exactly how he ran his life."

"He would have your hide for ever thinking about developing this into condominiums."

"He doesn't have anything to say about it and neither do any of you. 'Six orphans'...there's not one of you under six feet, Jody's in law school, Ryan's in medical school—"

This time she spun away from him, rifling through the unfamiliar cabinets. While dishes clattered and silverware jangled, Drew calmly walked to the correct cabinet and pulled out a saucepan, then ran the fillets under cold tap water.

"Stop it!" Holly actually stamped her foot. "Stop acting as though you know more about everything here than I do."

His voice was subdued, his eyes flashing with the effort. "I know more about this kitchen and more about this land, and before this is over, I'll see that you know all that too."

She glowered. "I have no intention of staying in this godforsaken town long enough to make it necessary."

Drew ignored her. "And if you're going to lock horns with us, then get us straight. Matt's the med student. He and Jody are the upwardly mobile types like you, and the bogs made it possible."

Holly gave him a look that said clearly she couldn't have cared less and marched past him, back to the parlor. He clomped after her in his waders, still talking.

"It's a family-run, family-owned business, built on sweat and determination." Before she could protest, Drew took her hands, turning them palms up. "You've never done a hard day's work in your life. You couldn't possibly know what it's taken to keep six kids together."

The intensity of Drew's feelings for his family stirred her, frustrated her. She flinched as he suddenly ran the tips of his fingers over her hand where calluses would have been. The sensation fragmented into a current that moved through her and she pulled her hand away.

Rubbing both palms over her woolen pants didn't help. She picked up her wineglass from the coffee table.

"Just because I lack an extensive callus collection doesn't mean I'm not acquainted with hard work, and just because I don't have brothers and sisters doesn't mean I don't have feelings."

Drew watched her gulp the aperitif. "You have feelings, all right. You're a jumble of repressed emotions that wouldn't have gotten in the way at all if you'd stayed in your safe little city. You've owned Bittersweet Bogs for six months. You've been cashing our loan payments for that long."

Holly looked at the fire and then at Drew, confused by the lack of animosity in his face as he continued. "One day we woke up and there were back-hoes doing perk tests, then surveyors arrived and jammed their little orange flags all over the place. You took care of the preliminaries quite nicely from your armchair in Philadelphia, Holly, but something made you come and see it for yourself. Guilt? Curiosity? Is this your swan song before the bulldozers chew it up? Maybe anger or just desire to see what your uncle kept from you . . ."

She opened her mouth, fury making her ears ring. "That's enough!"

"You're not going to win this one." A slight movement along his firm jaw was the only indication that he was restraining himself. "What's no more than added income to you is a way of life for us. It won't be changed on the whim of some resentful city mouse who hasn't even spent a week here."

He became thoughtful, still watching her, his eyes moving from her face up to the piled, toast-colored hair. She touched her comb self-consciously. "I'm just here to meet with the realtor and developer." It was an effort to put force in her words.

Drew's reply was close to a whisper. "We'll see. You've got a real fight on your hands, city mouse, and the fight's in here." He tapped the hollow of her throat and smiled when her breath caught. "In fact, it'll take so much energy, you may not have any left to fight the six of us."

"I told you last night—"

"You told us your intentions, your opportunities and your philosophies, dry and impersonal as the letterhead your attorney uses. I want to see gut reaction, I want to see you fired up about the future of Peter's land."

She was livid, speechless, as he pulled the glass from her fingers and took a swallow. "God-awful," he said. "I'm not surprised."

"What would you know about civilized drinks!"

"About as much as you know about your own emotions." On that note Drew moved to the foyer, then stood, making no move to leave while the tension nearly crackled the air in the thin space separating them. "Thirty-one in a couple of months, right?"

"What?"

"Kevin's thirty-six, Sean and I thirty-four, right down the line to Matt who's twenty-four. I figure you're between the six of us."

"Being *across* from the six of you was bad enough. I have no intention of getting *between* any of you."

He smiled and glanced at the stereo. "If you intend to play your uncle's opera records, keep your windows closed. My one regret is that we didn't have him buried with them. Come spring I don't want to hear Carmen tormenting Don José."

"I don't intend to be here in the spring."

"Neither will any condo owners." Six feet of adversary crossed his arms. "It's going to be a challenge convincing you of that."

Holly pulled her shoulders back. "May I ask exactly how you intend to change my mind?"

"It's been suggested that one of us grit our teeth, seduce you and marry you for the community property."

Holly was prepared for the grin but Drew blushed. She took half a step backward. "Over my dead body!" How could he dare choose that moment to look endearing!

"That was suggested, too." He was still studying her. "Still waters run deep. Five think you don't give a damn about anything but yourself and the money you stand to make. One of us, fool that he is, swears he's seen evidence of a human being behind those blue eyes, someone not quite as insensitive as she wants to appear."

"I suppose Matt is studying psychiatry?"

"Gastroenterology, actually."

Holly looked at her lacquered toes and put her hand on the doorknob. "Well, then, tell him to stick to his specialty." Her gaze moved up, over the waders, the duck call, the olive-drab jacket, to the expectant expression on the handsome face. "And you stick to yours, which is cranberries."

Drew's fingers went over Holly's, twisting the doorknob slowly until the night rushed in. Holly was grateful for the brisk intrusion, blaming the temperature for her trembling.

"Neighbor," he said finally, "change your taste in liquor, music, toenail polish and land development and

I'll come back to share the duck and some more of the Branigan insight.''

Holly picked up the wooden call from his chest, put it to her lips and blew. Its plaintive squawk closely resembled a Bronx cheer. Drew Branigan was still laughing as he stepped from the porch into the shadows and disappeared down the hill to his own house.

When Holly finished drinking her kir, she dropped the needle onto side two of the opera and stared into the flames, which were only slightly hotter than her own thoughts.

Drew's unwelcome insights jabbed like thorns long after he'd disappeared into the night. She didn't want any of them speculating about her. It *was* none of their business, and if she wanted to develop her property, neither was that.

Where was her professional distance? Why did it hurt so much to be hated by a blur of Irish masculinity when she hated them back? She reexperienced the same sense of resentment and hurt she had felt before in the recesses of her heart so many years ago. To a ten-year-old, the explanation that her beloved bachelor uncle had been the cause of her family's financial near ruin didn't seem reason enough for his desertion.

Holly remembered the time when Peter had left her family to live in Massachusetts. There he had found himself taking care of six suddenly orphaned children. One ten-year-old with two parents still alive seemed dust in the wind by comparison. Dust that didn't settle until her father moved them from New Jersey to Philadelphia—where a new school and new friends made her forget her father's ruined business, followed by her uncles' desertion. New ventures seemed successful, life was pleasant; Peter Bancroft was rarely mentioned and gradually forgotten.

Holly jammed another log on the fire while listening to the song of the clown Canio: *"Ridi, pagliacci..."* Laugh clown, laugh, and everyone will applaud. Laugh over your shattered love, she mentally translated.

There was a roar over the tortured Canio's voice. It was deep and as loud as a freight train and it scared Holly as badly as Drew's unexpected appearance at the door.

Holly swung herself around but the room hadn't changed; the roar wasn't coming from inside. "A plane's crashing," she whispered, and then calmed herself by thinking that no doubt there was something logical going on outside, something connected to the cranberry harvest on the Branigan bogs.

Holly slipped into her leather flats, hugged herself against the chill and went out the front door onto the porch. The roar was louder there, but the overhang from the roof blocked the view. Maples, pines and birches, thick along the side of the house, sheltered the sky as Holly walked through them, kicking the first of fallen leaves. It took no more than twenty seconds for her to reach open lawn, enough time for the hammering of her heart to leap tenfold. There was a logical explanation, and alone in the dark it made her scream. Her house was on fire.

Two

From the whitewashed chimney at the peak of the roof, blue flames shot into the night sky with a roar. It looked like a volcano, with embers the size of a man's fist dancing off the shingles, bouncing into the dry October foliage at Holly's feet. She stamped her thin shoes and muffled her screams.

She turned frantically in the direction of the Branigans' at the bottom of the hill. The house was dark with only a single floodlight shining from the eaves of the barn. They were gone.

She looked back at the chimney fire and then, knowing she shouldn't, went back into the house. It was as warm and cozy as she had left it, Placido Domingo and all. She called the Millbrook Fire Department, fully expecting the walls to blow out around her. When they didn't, Holly grabbed a wool blazer and went back outside to wait.

She huddled at the crest of the hill where a tangle of bittersweet hedge and holly bushes bordered the property, already hearing the distant sirens as the trucks worked their way through the village and out the state road. In another minute Holly heard the downshift of the laboring engines as they entered the lane separating Bancroft from Branigan, barely missing her parked BMW.

She turned her back on the fire long enough to watch the trucks approach. The whining sirens wound down, replaced by the crackle of the two-way radio. Men scrambled from the cab in full gear, two maneuvering the ladder as they swung it up onto the roof, two heading for the house with hand-held extinguishers.

Someone asked if she were alone, then told her to stay put. She did as she was told, shivering, jacket doubled over her rib cage. She shook as much from nerves as the cold, watching embers sail in the wind from the top of her uncle's house.

Holly bit her lip. If she had been more pleasant, Drew might have stayed. She put her head against her fist, nauseated from fear and curiosity, her gaze drawn to the roof, yet terrified one of the men would slip or that the shingles would burst into flames.

She thought of Domingo and the breasted duck, of the fine old tester bed, which the will said had been her great-grandmother's. While Holly prayed that Peter Bancroft's worldly possessions wouldn't be incinerated, the unfamiliar instinct to save what was newly hers washed over her. Holly opened her fists and cried, hating to loose what an hour earlier she had sworn she had no intention of keeping.

Peter Bancroft had been torn from her again. This time she would lose all physical evidence that her uncle

had existed. He'd been a man who had died so alien-
ated from his family that he'd never been told that he'd
outlived his brother by more than a year.

The first time, Holly, as a child, had buried her grief
in anger. This time, alone in the bittersweet vines, she
pulled woolen sleeves over the tears and called it fear.

Above her, a fire fighter continued to shoot the fine
spray from a hose attached to the tank on the truck.
Even at that distance she could hear him swear against
the steam it produced, as treacherous as the flames had
been.

The autumn night was clear, the Branigans' neat,
rambling farmhouse, gray under the harvest moon. In
the light from the barn she could see their pickup truck
and beyond the house the dark, geometric bogs, crimson in daylight, their cranberries ripe and ready for
picking.

The Branigans had amassed fifty acres of working
bogs spread over a two-hundred-acre area, which also
included woods, fields and ponds to flood the bogs. For
the second time that night Holly wondered why a devoted, supposed father figure hadn't left these men his
land and canceled their debt.

She turned back as a fire fighter came down the ladder. He walked past her, an ax in each hand on the way
to the house. "She's out," he called, "but stay put."

Her teeth were chattering as the fear worked itself
into helplessness, something she had fought against all
her life. The front door was open, *Pagliacci* still playing. *Di quel sdegno, e l'amor mio piu forte!* So angry
are you, so much stronger is my love!

A fire fighter came down the steps, told her the damage was minor and put his hand on her shoulder.
"Ma'am, we're going to have to open the wall next to

the fireplace. She's hot and there's a chance the lath will go. We'll pull as little plaster as possible and clean it up."

Holly's cheeks were still damp but she nodded. Canio, the tortured clown, met his demise as plaster dust rose in puffs in front of the parlor window. Ripping lath, the scrape of furniture on the pine floors, the sound of men working, all drifted to her from the house while the open channel of the fire truck radio crackled in the night air.

There was more crunching on the gravel driveway, another splash of headlights as a Ford Bronco bounced up next to the hook and ladder, but Holly's attention was caught by the sound of her name on the porch.

The tallest of the men called, "Holly" and pulled the helmet off his thick brown hair as he came to her. Her heart jumped as he then tugged away the mask from his ash and dust-encrusted face, leaving raccoon circles around his clear, green eyes.

"Drew!" There was enough composure and reserve in Holly's nature to keep her from throwing her arms around his neck, but not enough to prevent her leaning with relief into his heavy, protective jacket.

He put his gloved hand on her shoulder. "I'm Sean."

She stepped back, embarrassed, while he put his helmet back on and looked beyond her to his brothers. Drew and Kevin were coming from the Bronco. "Damn near threw her arms around me," he said to his twin. "Thought I was you. Things must have warmed up since last night."

Drew looked at the chimney. "Considerably."

"You all right?" Kevin asked.

Holly replied that she was, further embarrassed when she realized the question had been directed at Sean, who was nodding. "Chimney fire—a real bitch. Took Donald Sinnott twenty minutes to knock the creosote away. You know how much of it was built up in there?"

This time she was being addressed, but the question was rhetorical.

"Years. Ten more minutes and the wall would have gone. Peter should have had it cleaned, but you should have had more sense than to burn a fire first thing in a strange house, especially one as old as this."

Holly bit her lip. Kevin went up the steps as Drew's arm curved across her back. "Sean, you're being awfully hard on her."

The sooty face scowled. "The hell I am. Don nearly lost his eyebrows up there. Steam's worse than the flames."

"I'm really sorry. I didn't know." Her voice was small.

"There's a lot you don't know," Sean replied.

"You made your point and I've apologized for my stupidity," Holly snapped. She knew he was exhausted and she knew he was right. With a sigh she left the twins and went inside to look at the damage.

The fire fighters were filling garbage bags with remnants of thirty-year-old wallpaper, splintered lath and pieces of horsehair plaster the size of shovel heads. A fine dust filled the air and it smelled of wet wood and steamy heat.

The men trooped past her with the bags after explaining the extent of the damage, the need to have the bricks repointed and the chimney cleaned. Don Sinnott, who still had his eyebrows, shrugged off her apology and told her that's what they got paid for.

Obviously none of them is a Branigan, she thought, smiling at their kindness. She tried hard to keep the smile with lips that trembled. Loose chunks of wall still lay on the hearth. The braided rug and side chairs were shoved up against the couch, and the contents of the mantel were strewn on the coffee table. The one casualty, her goblet, lay shattered and unnoticed in the empty log carrier.

"This damage won't do much for the real estate value," Kevin said. He stood over her, an inch taller than Drew, his hair a shade lighter. Like the rest of them, a smattering of freckles across Celtic features made him appear far more congenial than he ever was. Holly pressed an index finger under her eyes, holding in tears, willing stoicism.

"Leave it till morning," Kevin continued. "For now you can stay with us."

Her eyes widened, her breasts rising as she straightened. "I wouldn't think of it! The fire's out. I'll be fine." She wasn't fine, and the last men on earth she wanted to be with stood on either side of her.

Drew wrapped his hand easily around her arm as she tried to kneel down on the hearth. "This is no time to be stubborn." His hunting attire had been replaced with fresh cords, a tartan shirt and down vest. Through the smell of dust she caught a wiff of after-shave and realized it was from his freshly shaved face. Had he been this warm when he had touched her earlier? Had her own hands trembled when she picked up the duck call?

Holly brushed at the white smudges on her pants, then looked at Drew. "I'm quite used to coping on my own. I don't need you," she added, meeting his eyes for emphasis.

Kevin broke the moment's spell. "There's an opening in your wall the size of a compact car." He looked across the foyer at the darkened doorway. "You sleeping down here in Peter's room? You've got no cats, house's been locked up for half a year. Three hours from now the mice'll be out and you'll lie in there alone in that bed thinking somebody's breakin' in.''

Alone in that bed . . . She didn't like his implication but all she said aloud was "Mice?"

"Squirrels, too, probably," Drew added. "Chew so loud you can hear the lath splinter."

"I've dealt with cockroaches and I can survive a wild mouse or two. You're just trying to frighten me." She drew herself up to her full five feet five. "Honestly, what do you think I am?"

Drew still held her arm. "A very spunky, badly frightened neighbor who could use a shower and a warm bed."

Kevin looked disgusted. "And no one's trying to scare you. There's no frost warning tonight; I just don't want a hysterical woman calling and disturbing what little sleep I get this time of year."

Drew gently extracted a stray bit of plaster from her hair. "I'll see she doesn't disturb your sleep." The two men laughed, but there was no meanness in it. At this point, Holly had grown to expect the Branigan blush that mottled the bridge of both noses.

Her scalp tingled where Drew's fingers had worked the debris from her hair. "You'd be the last men I'd call if I had mice or intruders. The police are as close as the phone, though with my luck one of you is a cop, too."

"Ryan, actually," Kevin said, grinning at her surprise. "Intermittent police officer, covering at the moment for one of the men out on disability. Works four-to-midnight shift."

"What!"

Kevin shrugged and started across the room. "We've gotcha covered, kid, not that any of us likes it any better than you do. Go get whatever it is you sleep in. I'm not known for my patience." He paused at the open front door and looked at his brother. "Drew, you're the one bringing strays home all your life. If you can't talk sense into her, just pick her up and carry her. I'll be in the car."

When he had gone, Drew looked back at her. "Forget trying to win the argument with Kevin, Holly."

"I will win."

"I meant staying with us."

"I didn't." The kir and the trauma and the air thick with dampness and smoke had made her nerves raw. She was fighting fatigue, fear and unwelcomed longing to let someone else take care of her, if only for the moment. When Drew put his hands on her shoulders, longing danced over those nerves like a squirrel across high-tension wires.

He moved his fingers to the sides of her face and she tilted her head. In the time it takes to inhale, she caught her breath against the depth of her physical response. She closed her eyes, her lips softening.

"You're expecting a kiss," he murmured.

Her eyes flew open and she blushed in fury. "I am not! I'm exhausted past thinking straight. I don't expect anything from you or your brothers. You're all a bunch of self-centered egomaniacs."

"Methinks she doth protest too much."

"Spare me the Shakespeare."

"Spare me *The Taming of the Shrew*; now get going. Kevin'll drag you out of here by your painted toenails even if I don't. Go get your toothbrush."

"Drew—"

"Move!"

"You are an arrogant, assuming, egotistical—"

His handsome face was split by his grin. "—gentleman who's about to go rifle through your underwear
drawer himself if you don't hustle, and lucky for you,
there are five more where I came from."

The ride was bumpy as Kevin backed the Bronco up
to the fork in the driveway and steered it toward home,
his home. Holly watched the shrubbery pass, washed in
the headlights, and tried to get used to the idea that she
was about to spend the night with two bachelors who
had nothing but contempt for her. She turned her head
from Kevin to Drew, both of whom were looking out
the windshield. Well, maybe only one of them felt contempt. Whatever Drew was feeling didn't make her any
less tense.

They wound their way down the slope to the neat
compound of the Branigans' buildings. The storage
shed and barn, garden outbuilding and farmhouse were
bright under the full moon. The house, white clap-
board and rambling, was lighted across one side. Next
to the pickup sat a sleek import.

"Jody's back," Kevin said.

Three bachelors; she felt a little queasy. "Exactly how
many of you will there be?"

Kevin killed the engine. "This is it. Matt's gone back
to school, Sean and his family are on the other side of
the pond and Ryan spends most of his time with his
girlfriend, Johanna."

Holly got out of the car trying to concentrate on the
small sense of relief; only three—could be worse. The
lighted windows belonged to the kitchen, which they
entered from the porch. There was a window box full of

end-of-the-season mums and a muddy pair of gum-soled boots at the stoop. The whitewashed, barnboard storm door was full of scrapes under the latch. Dogs, she thought; they probably raise packs of guard dogs and retrievers for hunting.

The kitchen was neat, cheerful and spotless with the exception of a cake pan next to the sink. Holly chided herself for being chauvinistic enough to have expected chaos. With the Branigans she was learning to expect the unexpected. She kept being hit over the head with it.

Kevin took her dusty blazer while Drew motioned for her to precede him into the family room. She lead the way past pegs hung with foul weather slickers, waders and old shirts. All of them, like their owners, seemed to be the same size, and Holly was struck again with the sense of unity—us against the world.

She entered the room with Drew behind her and glanced around the cozy space. There were masses of informal snapshots in small frames on a corner table, shelves filled with books and two large photographs over the couch. One, of the bogs in the fall, brilliant with floating berries, was balanced by a portrait of a mother and six fresh-faced boys. It tugged at Holly, all of it, but what stopped her in her tracks were the goings-on by the wood stove.

There were two lumps of sleeping fur, a black and a yellow one next to a naked, tanned back in the process of pivoting. A blonder version of Drew, toweling wet hair and holding a square of gingerbread in his teeth, matched Holly's startled expression with his own.

He uttered something she was grateful she couldn't understand, zipped the wide-open fly of his jeans and took the gingerbread out of his mouth. Droplets of water hissed as they hit the hot cast iron.

"You and your women, Drew! You could have called." The Branigan blush was vivid, but his composure was intact.

"It's only Holly, the phantom neighbor."

"I know perfectly well who she is," Jody shot back.

"I've had a fire," Holly added. "Your brothers insisted that I come over."

Jody looked at her and pulled on his shirt. "I know that, too. Saw the trucks leaving, talked to Sean. You'd think you'd know better, strange house and all."

Holly was unaware that she had stepped closer to Drew until they touched. He looked from her back to Jody. "Sean already let her have it; you can lay off. I should have thought to say something when I took her the duck."

"One of the ones you shot this afternoon?"

Drew nodded. "Peace offering. We were all a little rough on her."

"Come on," Jody said to his brother. "She's the one who plans to tear everything apart."

"You know," Holly finally interrupted, "I would appreciate it if you all would stop speaking as if I'm not here."

"You haven't been," Jody countered.

"Well, I am now and there's no point in rehashing this. I've got insurance claims and damage to think about, and if you don't mind I'd like to take a shower and go to bed without another argument."

"Be my guest," Jody said, finishing off the gingerbread. He looked at Drew. "I'm going out with Kevin to check the pump house; leave the door open."

When Drew told Holly to follow him, it may have been the first time since her arrival in Millbrook that she did what she was told without arguing with a Branigan. Together they left the brothers and the sleeping dogs and climbed the stairs.

The second floor consisted of a series of doors on either side of a wide dark hallway. Drew made no comment as to whose was whose until they reached the last one on the left. He snapped on a light and dropped her small piece of designer luggage on the chair. "Ryan's," he said as she looked at the remnants of school days, "and Matt's when he's here."

There was a set of bunk beds next to a desk; Drew pointed to the bottom. "Sheets are clean. I'll put towels in the bathroom. Jody'll be across the hall, Kevin and I have rooms and another bath at the front of the house. Take your shower and get some sleep. We'll see you in the morning. If there's any commotion, it's just us monitoring the bog temperatures, checking the sprinklers if there's a frost. Probably won't be tonight."

He turned reluctantly, as if leaving were an effort. "Any Irish in you?" he added.

Holly shook her head.

"You're a spunky little thing. Probably would have stayed over there by yourself if we'd given you half a chance."

"I would have been a wreck staying at Uncle Peter's by myself tonight," she said in a whisper, hating to admit it, but oddly relieved that she had. Her eyes blurred as she looked at him and she stood still until she was sure no tears would spill.

Drew came back to her. "Peter's house is yours, Holly. We all think of it as yours."

"Please don't."

The smile, which had never completely left, played at the edges of his mouth. "You're a lot more fun to drag home than wounded birds and abandoned pups, city mouse, though a damn sight more dangerous." As he spoke, his hands went back along her temples, thumbs stroking the edge of her hairline, as he had done in her parlor.

She tilted her face. "I'm not dangerous. I only want to come to a civil arrangement, to part as friends with all of you."

" ... The bluest eyes, innocent, sweetest face, mind like a steel trap, all covered with soot and ashes. There'll be no parting as friends. You can't have it both ways."

Holly touched her cheek, with fingers surprisingly cold as she thought about how she must look. His last words stung. This time she was sure he would drop his hands and go; she wanted him to go. Which is why when he bent his head and kissed her, she gasped.

"What are you doing?" came from her throat in a tremulous whisper.

"Giving you the kiss you expected a while ago, driving you wild with passion, making you helpless with desire. To be perfectly honest, I'm going to do it again."

Holly Bancroft stood on tiptoes in Drew Branigan's house and let herself be kissed senseless. He expects me to protest, to scream and carry on, she thought with what brain cells were still functioning. Wild with passion, maybe ... helpless with desire? Never! She would never be helpless.

Her mental monologue began to fuzz over, the sentences dissolving into impressions, impressions to sensations, physical sensations. She felt the texture of his hair between her fingers, the tightness in his chest where her breasts touched his shirt. The wool on her thigh scratched as he pressed against it. Somebody moaned, she wasn't sure who, but as his hand slid along the side of her ribs, she pulled away. She pulled the zippered suitcase from the chair a little too fast, and held it to her with both hands. "I'm going to take a hot bath," she said to Drew's shoe tips. "I suggest you try a cold shower."

She left the room so quickly that she could still feel the pressure of his mouth on her lips as she yanked on the faucets, deciding at the last minute that a shower might do her some good, too.

She hung her nightgown on the back of the door, dropped everything she was wearing in a heap and stepped behind the frosted glass. Seduced, community property...she scrubbed her scalp. What did a man, raised by a man and one of six brothers, know about a woman? Obviously nothing, she answered to herself not the least bit troubled that her body still hummed.

Holly was in the process of turning off the water when she remembered her host had implied there were no fresh towels. The spray stopped; it wouldn't kill her to use Ryan's. She slid the glass door back on its track as her hand splayed unconsciously across her breasts. Her discarded clothes were gone from the floor but one woolen pant cuff peeked from the lid of the wicker hamper. On top was a neatly folded bath sheet and face towel. Her head spun to the door, but it was as she had left it, closed. Under the pressure of her fingertips, her heart resumed its pounding. Okay, okay, she should have known better than to try for the last word. Next time she'd lock the door.

Holly toweled dry her hair. What was she thinking! There'd be no next time.

Strange sounds in a strange house wouldn't keep her up and neither would strange men. When her shoulder-length hair was blown dry and the rest of her rubbed briskly with the terry cloth, she tiptoed back to the bedroom and snuggled into the fresh sheets on the bottom bunk. The house was still. All the brothers, she guessed, were out at the sprinklers. No matter what her host cared to believe, the strongest feeling flowing through her was fatigue. Though it was barely ten o'clock, Holly fell soundly, dreamlessly asleep.

She awoke in a blur, however, startled by some internal alarm. The dark room was partially lit by a shaft of gray light from the hallway. Blocking most of it was a figure she thought she'd recognize across a bog, let alone across a room.

Her fright was softened by anger at his presumption. She ignored the brief thrill as it shot through her. "Drew Branigan," she hissed, "stop this adolescent sexual behavior and go back to your own bed!" She sat up, covers tumbling to her waist as her hair tangled in the slats supporting the mattress above her.

There was a streak of blue language, the flick of a lamp and six feet two inches of uniformed police officer was made manifest. The look in Holly's saucer-sized eyes flew from the badge to the gun belt to the blue stripe along his pant leg as he squatted to her level.

"Well, well, Goldilocks," Ryan said, "May I ask what you're doing in my bed?"

"Drew!" It was not so much a plea as an alarm, bringing within seconds a black Labrador retriever, a golden Labrador retriever, Jody, Kevin and—pushing them all aside—Drew, himself. With the exception of the police officer who was still squatting at the edge of the mattress, no one had on much more than a shocked expression.

Three

———

Holly yanked her hair free with one hand as the other drew a fistful of blanket to her collarbone. She got to her feet but tripped over Ryan's black, uniform dress boots as both dogs barked and yapped.

"Call off these animals," she cried indignantly into the blanket, avoiding the swirl of bare chests, boxer shorts and pajama bottoms at the doorway.

"Ryan," Drew snapped, "Jody, Kevin, get out!" He was actually laughing.

"I mean it," she cried. Drew finally tugged each dog by the collar. "I should have known better than to spend one minute in this overaged fraternity house. Your juvenile attempts at intimidation won't work." Her voice was clear and forceful, hampered only by the failed attempt at stern dignity. She pulled Ryan's Hudson's Bay blanket tighter against her Vanity Fair nightgown, but the end was still tucked in and it started to hike up her leg. They were all looking at her polished toenails.

Jody stepped forward and she flinched but he reached past her for the dogs. Drew let go of them, gesturing them away casually, looking as though he were accustomed to parading around in front of her half dressed.

Kevin, also in underwear, muttered something about hysterical women and swept them all with a look. "You work this out," he said to Drew. "Ryan, the next time you plan to use your own bed, call first, damn it."

"Call! I live here. How the hell should I know you'd put the blonde in my bed? When did we ever need a guest room?"

Holly clutched the blanket and sheet around her. "You must know I've had a fire. I'll be gone in the morning." Kevin left; two to go. Ryan sat down at the desk, pulling off his boots.

"What are you doing?" She looked from the police officer to Drew who was retying the cord to his pajama bottoms. Her eyes flew from his fingers to his face, bouncing off the muscled chest on the way up. He was grinning, so she spun back to Ryan, who was now working on the gun belt.

"I'm getting ready for bed. Of course I know about the chimney fire. I just never thought—"

"I was led to believe you'd be with Joanne tonight," Holly interrupted.

A look passed between the remaining brothers. "Johanna. True love never runs smooth."

Drew was now lounging against the doorframe, his arms crossed across his chest. As Ryan put the gun and holster on the desk, Holly swept past him, the sheet and blanket trailing as if she were a child playing monarch.

As she got to the door, Drew reached to touch her. "Holly—"

She flinched again. "You have a couch downstairs. I'd just as soon be a floor away from all of you, anyway."

"Stubborn little thing," Ryan sighed, unpinning his badge. "But I guess we knew that. Still an empty bed in here. You're wearing most of it, in fact."

Holly didn't bother to answer, caught instead by a sudden welling of emotion. Drew's lips parted to reply, but Holly found her voice as she glared at him. "If you make one more fresh remark, you'll get a healthy jab of Bancroft elbow in your solar plexus. It should be perfectly obvious by now that I would rather be anywhere but in this Irish roadhouse, and as soon as humanly possible I'll be gone. To Philadelphia," she added as though there might be any doubt. "Now if you'll let me by, your brother can take off what's left of his uniform and I can go downstairs."

Drew stepped from her path. "Forget the couch," he said softly. "Go on down to my room. You can have my bed."

"What?"

"Don't panic, I have no intention of joining you. My masochistic tendencies stop with trying to earn a living from cranberries. I'll take the bottom bunk."

Her eyes narrowed but she let him ease her out of the room and down the hall. A small light glowed from the bedside table and the double bed was a heap of disheveled comforter. "I left in a hurry," he explained chuckling.

Drew's room was large and as full of personality as he was, all of which she tried to ignore. She stood next to the bed, still wrapped in the covers. "This was my parents' room,'' he offered as though the size needed explanation. ''And then Peter's when he moved over here during those years.''

She moved her head in a half nod, glancing from his clothes on the bedpost to the play of light on his chest. She hoped her expression said clearly that she didn't want to hear about Peter Bancroft playing father.

Drew stopped talking and took another step toward her—again she flinched. His features were totally expressive; in an instant the amusement fell away, replaced by concern. As much as she hated being buffeted by the rest of them, she resented Drew's instinctive protectiveness and the waves of gratitude that rippled through her in response. It almost felt like affection.

He pointed to a small wooden box on the table. ''I was only reaching for the monitor. The digital readout is the bog temperature and there's an alarm, which will go off if frost is threatening, so we can flood. Hold still. I'm just going to turn it off so it doesn't wake you. Kevin has the same setup in his room.''

Holly moved to the side. ''I suppose I did overreact a little...to everything.'' It was the closest she could come to an apology.

''It was funny, you must admit,'' Drew said.

''What was? Ryan? Your dogs? The fire? How about the towels appearing in the bathroom!'' she added, glaring into the innocent, green eyes.

''We couldn't have you dripping down the hall.''

''I would have managed. I can take care of myself quite nicely. I've been doing it for years.''

''So you keep telling me.''

Holly watched him fiddle with the monitor. Looking at him was a pleasure, except that he had a disconcerting way of looking back at her as if her thoughts were printed on her face.

"You know, Drew, I'm well aware that you and your brothers are purposely trying to keep me off guard. The only reason you've been mildly successful this far is because I'm not used to—"

"Men."

"I didn't say that." The pit of her stomach was tightening.

"We're an unpredictable bunch. You'll have to get used to that."

"I don't intend to be here long enough to have to," she answered abruptly. For a moment they stood staring at each other in the low light and sudden silence.

"No," Drew added, "Philadelphia is waiting. You keep telling me that, too. Although you certainly didn't kiss me tonight as though you had anything waiting in Philadelphia."

She gave him her best smile. "Perhaps I can be unpredictable, too." She was treading on thin ice. "It's one of the little rituals we women enjoy." She was also enjoying the obvious effort it was taking Drew to keep his eyes on her face as she unwrapped the blanket and sheet he needed.

"Sleep well," she added, handing him the bundle.

"You, too," he said taking the blanket in his right arm, his left sliding down her back. Holly's breath caught at the sensation of cool nylon against Drew's warm smooth skin and the rough wool blanket. "Shall I tuck you in?" he managed.

She stepped back, sinking onto the bed. "No!"

"You're right, we might start another fire." He smiled and lowered his eyes, catching every nuance of the flush rising from the bodice of Holly's nightgown along her throat and into her ears. "And one of us is nearly in flames already," he whispered, kissing her with parted lips.

She had raised her head as he bent down but she stayed seated on the edge of the bed, her hands full of bunched percale to keep them from caressing his shoulders. My God, she thought, what am I doing half-naked in Drew Branigan's bed! When he straightened, she snapped off the light and dived into the depths of his comforter.

The laugh that followed her was deep. "Sleep well," he added.

"I intend to," she muttered into his pillow. She lay in the dark aching for Drew and aching for the tangible Branigan hostility, which kept all those other trouble-some emotions at bay. This small bit of hospitality offered because of the bond Peter Bancroft had cemented, would be quickly forgotten once they got back to the business at hand. She'd see to it.

Groggy with fatigue, Holly slept unmoving until the sensation of flannel on her bare arm made her stir. The covers rose from her breasts up to her chin and a ten-dril of hair slid across her cheek to be tucked behind her ear.

The room was gray in the half light of dawn. Holly blinked, too warm and comfortable to raise her head, heard nothing and went back to sleep. Three hours later she awoke to full daylight and intimate surroundings. The room was cluttered with photographs, stacks of books and beautiful furniture. There was correspon-dence on the desk and a discarded sweater on the chair. A suit in its cleaner bag hung on the closet doorknob; Drew Branigan dressed up occasionally. A fluttery rush of pleasure surprised her, and she felt embarrassed, as if she'd been caught blatantly invading someone's privacy. She sat up. The post where his clothes had been was empty and her suitcase sat on the blanket chest at the foot of the bed. She touched the hair now tucked behind her ear. Drew's pajamas were in a heap at the foot of the bed.

Holly didn't open the door until she was fully dressed, right down to sweater and socks. She tiptoed to the farthest bathroom, half expecting another assault of masculinity, but the second floor was quiet. Bedroom doors were open.

She splashed her face with cold water in an effort to get her thoughts back on track, then pulled yesterday's clothes out of the Branigan hamper and wrapped them in the cleaner bag from Drew's suit. When her overnight case was packed she straightened the bed, ignoring the pajama bottoms, and finally glanced out the windows. The bogs were bright in the morning sun, the first one flooded for harvesting. The mirror finish of the still water reflected the sky and the deep green boundary of piney woods to the south. The edge of the geometric field was crimson, however, lined with the thousands of berries, which had floated from their vines and were waiting to be corralled.

She raised her eyes, catching a rainbow in the spray from the sprinklers flooding the bogs beyond and then looked at the heavy equipment parked along the dikes. Branigan Cranberries was barely visible on the flatbed trailer, and she caught sight of one of the brothers working the water reel-picker down the ramp.

Memories she no longer knew she carried jammed Holly's head. Dry picking, neatly piled boxes to crate them, flatbed pickup trucks lettered with Bancroft, her uncle and her father and their seasonal workers pulling in a harvest in southern New Jersey. How old had she been the year she and her mother helped—nine? Ten? With deliberate calm Holly placed her open hands on Drew's windowsill, stunned by the depth of her response.

Her mother was crying—or Peter was. Holly squinted, no longer seeing the Branigans. No, it wouldn't have been Peter—he was supposed to have been the one funneling off the profits; her mother must have found out. Holly the child was patting them both...

There had been a pumpkin, too. Uncle Peter had carved it with her while they sat on the dike at lunch. It was a wonderfully mean jack-o'-lantern and her hands were gooey with the seeds and pulp. Peter hugged her goodbye with tears in his eyes. Peter *had* been crying and she had wanted to hug him back, but she was covered with pumpkin right up to her elbows.

Holly blinked, her fingers were white from pressing the sill. That autumn day was the last time she'd seen her uncle. Oh, God, what subconscious insanity had made her choose October to sell off his property? There was no rush. She was getting by on her trust fund and Kevin's loan payment. It wouldn't have felt so bitter in the spring; even school could have waited until then. Holly had wanted only to come to this hated place Peter Bancroft had chosen and liquidate it, take what it was worth and go home. She turned from the window. She didn't want the memories or anything to do with the men who stood in the way. She deserved the happiness the sale would make possible.

Holly moved quickly and quietly on the carpeted stairs, not stopping until the sound of her name drifting up from the first floor office made her pause on the landing. Her hand tightened on the banister.

"Helpless—don't be a fool, Drew. You haven't got the time no matter what you feel for the house." There was no mistaking Kevin's voice and no mistaking Drew's reply.

"She's a Bancroft; she's part of Peter. We owe him that much."

"Christ, Drew, every one of us is more kin than she is. Blood is thinner than water in this case."

"Kevin, let me work on her. She just got here."

"Work on her," Holly repeated to herself as a chair scraped over the wooden floor. There was a pause and she tried to decide whether it was safe to continue down the stairs.

"I can be very persuasive," Drew said, a remark that made her narrow her eyes and grit her teeth.

"I know all about your technique. Don't make the mistake of assuming all this stray needs is a dish of warm milk. Her claws are drawn, Drew, and so are the boundaries."

Drew's reply was muffled and she heard them leave the room. When the urge to strangle both of them had passed, she followed, wanting only to pick up her blazer and get out.

Drew was at the kitchen counter pouring a cup of coffee. "Good morning. Hope you're hungry," he said, pulling a second mug from the shelf.

"No, thank you. I'll eat at Uncle Peter's."

"Uncle Peter's," he repeated. "Can't you just call it your house?"

"It isn't my house."

"As a matter of fact, it is. You may not like the idea, but until you sign a bill of sale, it's yours—your bogs, your fields, your house. You're the one who keeps pounding that into me, so let's call a spade a spade, okay?"

When Holly didn't answer, he cocked his head and watched her expression. "Now, city mouse, I was just about to pour you a dish of warm milk so sit down and stay for breakfast."

Her eyes widened. "You jerk. You knew I was on the stairs."

"Goodness, you're sounding more like one of us all the time." He put a filled plate on the table with her mug next to it. "Now, you can be stubborn and march back up the hill out of principle or you can eat what Ryan made and be gracious about it. The rest of us finished hours ago."

"I don't want anything from any of the Branigans."

Drew's smile was a little forced. "We won't count a couple of cranberry muffins and two strips of bacon. If you intend to keep up this fight, I suggest you dig in to keep up your strength." He took his coffee and walked past her to the door, as she reluctantly sat down. She watched as he worked his faded jeans into knee-high work boots and then pulled a fisherman's knit sweater over his head. When the dark, disheveled hair appeared, it topped another grin.

"You have a tendency to turn all warm and soft when I get within three feet of you," he said, sipping his coffee and enjoying her anger. "That is, once you stop flinching. The only time you don't jump is when you're sound asleep."

Holly chomped on a piece of bacon. "I won't be the butt of your juvenile humor. I don't want your cock-eyed hospitality and I certainly didn't need tucking in at dawn."

Drew shrugged. "Old habits, hard to break—comes from checking my little brothers all those years, I guess. That and having to go to work in something besides the bottoms of my pajamas."

"Stop baiting me. I'm not going to sit here and talk about you in pajamas."

"How about you in nightgowns?"

Her blue eyes narrowed. "Don't you have cranberries to farm?"

"Pick" he corrected, "or harvest. The term is cranberry grower, not farmer."

"I don't care."

Drew touched her hair. "I think you do, Holly. I think even considering the possibility of caring scares you to death. You're floundering in a lot of muddy water at the moment, but the silt's going to settle, the water's going to clear. You've come to Millbrook for a reason."

"You know nothing about it!" She started to get up from the table, but Drew put his hand on her shoulder.

"I know everything about it and I know enough to back off. Finish your breakfast. I've got a full week ahead of me, and that doesn't even include teaching a dewy-eyed blonde about her heritage."

"My father only invested...my father was a banker," she called after him, but Drew had gone. Holly stayed long enough to finish breakfast, rinse the plate and stick it in the dishwasher. Beyond the kitchen window two brothers worked, knee-high in the watery bog, walking wooden corrals around the berries, feeding them onto the conveyor belt, which pulled them up into the back of a wooden-sided truck. Drew stood on the dike next to a pile of wet hulls.

Drew, she thought, and Kevin full-time growers. One a fire fighter, one a police officer, a law student and a future physician...all pulling together against frost and freezing, against time and against outsiders who threatened to change what they held sacred. She felt like one of the berries, surrounded by a Branigan corral, being herded in a direction she didn't want to go.

Holly shook her head, pulled her blazer from the peg and marched back up the hill to face her own problems.

Four

Holly was unlocking the door when the sound of tires on the gravel made her turn her head. A man in a business suit, carrying a briefcase, approached her briskly, hand outstretched.

"Miss Bancroft? I'm Charley Simms, your uncle's insurance agent."

Holly blinked. "Simms and Stone in Millbrook? I was just going to call—"

He was nodding, waiting for her to finish. "Yes, well I got the call about the fire last night. Like to move right ahead with these things."

"The call?" She ushered him into the clutter and debris.

"From Drew Branigan. We insure them, as well. Peter saw to that, of course. A great man, I might add, greatly missed. Did wonderful things for those boys."

"So I understand," she sighed. "I'm planning to sell this property, and I'd like it understood that I'll be taking care of things, including claims for this fire, myself. I hope you can expedite it for me."

"Certainly." He glanced at the damage, poking into the gaping hole next to the fireplace, and listened to Holly's explanation of what the fire department had recommended.

"It seems to be cosmetic except for the brick work," she said, depressed at the thought of restoring the room.

"Lucky thing. It would be a real shame to lose the character in this old place." He ran his hand over the dentil work on the mantel. "Can't even duplicate moldings like these anymore. The house's been here longer than the bogs, I suspect. In any case, your friends down the hill can give you the names of some craftsmen to match this plaster and repoint the brick."

He busied himself with the paperwork and handed her his card. "Get estimates from the carpenter and mason and have them give me a call. Should take about three days to settle. We'll wrap this up in no time."

Holly nodded while he took a handful of instant snapshots. His smile was reassuring. "Looks just awful now, but it won't take much. Chimney fires are more of a mess than anything else. We see half a dozen every year. Have a licensed sweep give it a good cleaning, too."

When the agent was finished, Holly walked him to the car, enjoying the warmth of the October sun. Deep furrows indented the lawn where the fire trucks had parked, but as she stooped to look at them another vehicle arrived. We Kleen It was stenciled on the side of a white van along with a phone number and Millbrook address. This time four men got out, two wearing industrial overalls. The driver smiled and handed her a business card.

"Tony Carvelli." He pumped her hand. "Sorry we're late—had to get a second van."

"Late?" Holly watched them pull supplies from the back. An industrial vacuum cleaner was followed by buckets of bottles and sponges.

"Drew Branigan said nine-thirty. It's after ten."

"You have the wrong house. The Branigans' is down the hill."

Tony strode toward the house while she dogtrotted next to him. "Chimney fire? Insured by Simms and Stone? They'll foot the bill under your homeowner's policy. No mistake. Drew don't make mistakes."

"Mr. Carvelli—"

He finally stopped but it was only to wait for Holly to open the door, which she did with a sigh. "Come in. The damage is in the parlor, obviously."

Tony raised a finger. "Only damage that's obvious to you. Smoke's got everywhere. We'll do the house, top to bottom. Better have things in the closets cleaned, too. Smoke'll rot fabric."

"The closets are empty. The house hasn't been lived in for some time. I'm just here to sell it," she replied, feeling swept by a tide of events over which she had little control.

Within minutes the house was alive with the hum of the vacuum and rug shampooers. The door to Peter Bancroft's bedroom had been closed, and though there were traces of dust, there was no damage. Holly ran a cloth over the furniture herself and then unpacked the few things she had taken with her to the next-door neighbors. She was living out of a suitcase, which was lying on top of an empty blanket chest under the win-

dow. Her dirty clothes went into the washing machine
in the mud room off the kitchen, and she spent the better part of the morning running Peter's curtains and
sheets through a wash and then the dryer. She found a
nautically wound clothesline on the shelf with the de-
tergent, and after noticing hooks imbedded in two
backyard maple trees, she fastened the line and air-
freshened the quilt and blankets.

Around her, fall color was at its peak. From the hill
she could see over the tops of the pines bordering her
uncle's bogs and out well to the east where Plymouth
Bay lapped the Massachusetts shoreline. She ignored the
view to the north where her neighbors were still pushing the cranberry harvest into the elevator.

During lunch a finish carpenter called to say he'd be
out the next morning to look at the job and gave her the
number of a mason who would be needed first. Holly
Bancroft was no longer surprised when the chimney
sweep telephoned. In fact, she told him she'd been
expecting to hear from him.

The surprise was that she didn't hear from Drew. At
four o'clock when We Kleen It left she stood in the
quiet, medicinal-smelling house alone. Damp rugs were
drying, shelves glistened, newly laundered linens were
back on the bed.

At five she opened the refrigerator she'd stocked, ignored the duck fillets and made herself a hamburger.
Tomorrow the tradesmen would put the rest of the
house back in order and she'd get on with the business
at hand. Holly munched her dinner on the couch,
looking around the room. An empty desk sat in the
corner, no doubt where the Bancroft papers had been
kept. Six months ago all those papers had been for-
warded to Philadelphia, and were now in the hands of

an attorney Holly had retained to deal with them. The box on the floor next to the chair hadn't been touched.

Holly sighed. Chimney sweeps, carpenters, masons... it would be impossible to supervise the repairs from Pennsylvania and foolish to go home only to return again to meet with the realtor. She hadn't packed enough clothes for more than a week, but lack of clothes was her only reason to go home. She could stay in middle-of-nowhere Millbrook forever and no one would mind.

It was dark when she washed her dishes. Nothing had been mentioned about staying another night down the hill and since she hadn't heard from any of them, Holly told herself she was glad she'd made her feelings clear.

No one called, no one left towels in her bathroom while she showered, and she awoke the next morning in the same position in which she'd fallen asleep, her covers untouched. Where was her sense of relief?

Eben Howard, the carpenter, was her first visitor. He discussed the virtues of plaster board versus real plaster, the expense and time involved and the philosophy of restoration as opposed to reproduction. She listened, thinking of her chrome and glass decor at home, and took his estimate.

The mason arrived in the afternoon, inspected the bricks and simplified everything by agreeing to repair the damage within the next twenty-four hours. Holly was beginning to feel the days slipping through her fingers, hours passing with little to do except focus on the personality still alive in the rooms around her. Nothing would be presentable for the realtor for probably another week, and she'd been fighting ghosts in the warm, antique house for three days already. The Boston firm was waiting for her call and, lordy, how she wanted to make it and just get out.

From the front bedroom she looked at the sun shining above the tops of the trees and then put on *Rigoletto*. It was Pavarotti this time, and she sat listening until there was a knock at the kitchen door. Holly walked through the house to answer it. The leap of emotion in her chest was so violent that she couldn't tell whether she was thrilled that it was Drew or aghast.

Drew was holding an orange, a bag of bread crumbs and a bottle of Grand Marnier. As usual, he was smiling, looking freshly scrubbed and for all the world as though he'd been invited to dinner. He cocked his ear. "Every time I come over here, someone's dying in Italian."

It made her smile. Too much of what he did made her smile. "Not yet," she replied. The tenor voice soared. "'Woman is fickle, like a feather in the wind...always changing her mind...'"

"Then there's hope," said Drew.

"I was only translating."

"Poor Gilda, seduced and abandoned." He put his armload on the counter.

Holly looked at him sharply. "But avenged."

"But she still wound up in a sack being dragged to the river."

"Well, well, for someone who professes to hate opera, you certainly seem to know the libretto."

Drew pulled the fillets from the refrigerator and closed the door with his shoulder. "I gave Peter that record a couple of Christmases ago," he said quietly.

There was another stab of emotion. "How thoughtful."

Drew shrugged. "Peter's idea of bedtime stories for Matt and Jody were the comedies; he saved the tragedies for working the bogs. All we wanted was a little rock music on Saturday afternoons..."

"And instead you got Milton Cross and the Metropolitan Opera!"

Drew looked at her shrewdly. "Only you would know that. It must be in the genes."

She was still smiling, watching him rummage through the kitchen drawers. "I take it you think you're staying for dinner?"

"We can't have you ruining that duck. I picked up the recipe from a great little restaurant in Plymouth. Matter of fact, you play your cards right and I'll take you there one of these days."

She watched his hands as he set things in place, which was less disturbing than watching his face. "Drew, I'm not sure you should stay for dinner."

There was a barely discernible change in his expression. "Don't trust yourself, hmm?"

"We'll just wind up fighting again."

"Fighting is what you're afraid of?"

She finally looked up into the warm, green eyes. "I'm not afraid of anything."

"Good. Then it's settled. Go set the table. Peter had candles in the left-hand drawer of the lowboy."

"Candlelight? Is that one more version of warm milk in a dish? You should listen to Kevin. I'm not some stray who's going to lap this up."

Drew buttered a baking dish. "Your tough act might have worked for a day or two, but the fire, thank God, worked in my favor. I've got a few extra days, a week if I'm lucky." He stuffed the duck and sprinkled the liqueur over it. "I watched you looking at those ashes two nights ago, stunned to think it could hurt so much to lose what you're pretending to hate."

She still hadn't left the kitchen. "You're being very melodramatic. I was terrified, of course. There was no one here for one thing and the damage might play havoc with the real estate value. Did that ever occur to you?" She left the room, marching past the lowboy into the parlor. Drew followed with his hands still covered with butter and bread crumbs.

Holly pointed to the damage. "This is what scared me, what it could mean in terms of the sale. And while we're at it, I suppose you want a thank-you for all the help you've been. For two days it's been a steady stream of insurance agents, cleaners and carpenters."

"Dinner with me will be thanks enough."

Holly looked at him as if she wished he meant it. "I don't want you taking care of everything."

"Tends to obligate you?"

She looked at his messy hands. "Don't you have a dinner to finish? Better still, how about a bog to pick or temperatures to monitor?"

"This work is just as pressing," he said with easy laughter.

"Yes, well, I'd appreciate it if you'd stop pressing, please." She led the way back to the kitchen trying not to enjoy the way Drew sounded when he was enjoying himself. She wanted to fuel another argument so she could get back to an emotion she recognized. Anger was honest and clean, not stimulating and confusing. Being in the same room with Drew Branigan was like drinking too much champagne. She was light-headed and always felt as though she had to choose her words carefully.

For the moment there were no words. She worked on a salad while he filled a pan for rice, the silence more comfortable than their words had been. He glanced occasionally at the doorway in the direction of the music and finally blurted, "Turn that thing off, will you?"

"You don't need to be rude. It's almost over and you might enjoy it if you give it a try. Uncle Peter probably told you the same thing."

She caught the clenching of jaw muscles and the sweep of lashes. "Holly—"

"Besides, as we all know, it's my house. A little culture might do you some good," she added.

"I was wrong. It's not your house, not yet. It's still Peter's; he's everywhere. No one played those damned records but him. It's as though he's in another room and he'll join us any minute."

Her heart froze. "Drew—"

"Yesterday when I looked up the hill and saw stuff hanging on the line, I had to look twice. Kevin nearly caught himself in the reel."

"Good Lord, why didn't you come over and say something?"

He straightened and washed his hands. "Because it's over and done, even if we're all a little raw still." He looked again toward the music. "I hadn't heard that since I found him." He turned his head and looked at her, into her eyes. "Your resemblance to him is incredible, you know."

She was caught between his need to talk and her dread of hearing any more. She left the room and put the album away, taking more time than she needed finding innocuous background music on the radio. It filled the air and eased her awkwardness. When she got back to the kitchen, Drew was putting the baking dish into the oven. "Thank you" was all he said.

She touched his arm, one of the few personal gestures she'd initiated. "Peter Bancroft has been lost to me for twenty years. He moved out of my life and into yours a long time ago, long enough for me to bury anything I felt. That doesn't mean I'm completely insensitive to what you must have gone through, but it's no use trying to get my sympathy."

"Sympathy—empathy—is where things might start to make sense. Isn't that why you've come back, to make sense out of all this?"

The truth when Drew spoke it was no more palatable than the half lies she'd been dishing out in self-defense. "Maybe," she sighed, "partly, but only for the two or three days it would take to arrange for the sale. That's the truth. I wanted to see it but I wanted to see it alone. To make this a clean break from a past full of..." she sighed again, looking for the right word.

"Shadows," Drew supplied.

Holly arched her eyebrows. "Shadows. He made a lot of people very unhappy. Look at you, the six of you. What would it take to sever a relationship as close as brothers?"

Drew moved from the oven, brushing her hair back in a gesture she was growing to expect. He played the ends over his fingers. "You tell me, Holly."

"My father and he were brothers and partners. Peter took advantage of it. He mishandled my father's investment in him. It was a breach of ethics as well as a breach of trust."

"Adult words for a child's perception."

"You've made it clear that you'll try anything to get me to change my mind, but dredging this up will only drive me out faster. Don't try to manipulate me."

"Why? Because you're beginning to see how much other people already have? You're a beautiful, intelligent woman capable of seeing things for what they are, not for what others would have you believe. Don't look so shocked. I'm not a magician who's going to cast a spell so you'll wake up tomorrow loving this. All I can do is make you see it, understand it. The love will come in time, and now, thanks to years of built-up creosote in that old chimney, that's exactly what I've got."

She backed away and her hair fell on her shoulder. "How can you be so sure?"

"Because there's been precious little love in your life. You're starving for it, city mouse, and when you find it, whether it be in a man or a job or a slice of God's green earth, it's going to knock your socks off."

She turned from him and wiped the counters with a sponge, then wrung it savagely in the sink. Drew opened a cabinet. "Peter's unopened Scotch still in here, or would you like another god-awful kir?"

She tried to focus on the change of subject. "Do you know every nook in this stupid house?"

"Of course. Who do you think cleaned out the belongings, Holly? Food spoils when it's left for six months. Creditors call for payment..."

"They told me... the attorney told me all that was taken care of by someone," she stammered.

"True enough. You're lookin' at him." He poured himself two fingers of Scotch. "How long's John Bancroft been gone?"

"A year and a half."

Drew shrugged and raised their glasses. "We're due, you and I."

She gave him a tentative look. "I'm not sure I like the sound of that."

"You and I? It has a certain ring."

They stood against the kitchen counters, nothing in the air but the sweet orange smell of dinner and the clink of ice against glasses. The strains of an orchestrated movie theme went unnoticed.

"Put on your jacket," Drew said suddenly. "We're losing daylight and I want to show you something."

"Now?"

"Now."

When they were out on the porch, Drew looked down the hill toward the Bancroft bogs. "Have you seen the orchard?"

"Orchard—you mean the trees next to Peter's bogs?"

"Aha, I knew you'd been paying attention."

"Of course," she sniffed. "I like to know what I'm selling." Holly hesitated as Drew took her hand and then tucked her arm into his.

He grinned his grin. "Chilly."

"Right."

Drew Branigan wasn't chilly, he was warm in all the places she brushed as they walked along the back of her property and out to Peter's bogs. In the dying light she looked at the flat, crimson plantings. "I hope it isn't too late to offer you the harvest."

He tugged her hand, pulling her to her knees at the edge of the dike and then taking a handful of vine in his fingers. "Lesson number one: the leaves have turned but there aren't any berries. They got Black Frost last winter. Peter wasn't well; we had a heavy snow. Photosynthesis stops when sunlight can't get through. Lost the crop.''

She looked at his hands. "The whole thing?"

"Berries never set in the spring. We were out here more nights than I like to remember, but we lost it, anyway."

Holly watched him in the low, yellow light as streaks of sunset filtered through a birch tree. "It can be that fragile? Peter didn't have a sprinkler system?"

"Pump's shot. Six-acre loss."

"Which translates into how much?" Holly asked.

"Sixty thousand dollars." Drew got to his feet. "We're here to see the orchard," he added, slapping one of the orange property markers. They continued along the dike to the neatly spaced fruit trees lining the far side of the bogs.

"MacIntosh," he added when they reached the trees. The ground was strewn with the apples, most lying buried in the shaggy grass. Holly leaned back against a trunk. "We planted these, all of us. Matt wasn't even as tall as the shovel we used and now the trees are full-grown, and the apples rotting."

Holly leaned harder as Drew pressed an open palm on the bark at her shoulder. "Mice'll gnaw the bark this winter, nest in the grass if it isn't cut away from the trunks. Deer'll be here, too, if we get much snow. Ever seen the damage hungry deer can do?"

She shook her head.

"Ever smelled a kitchen when apple butter's been made? Ever put up enough for toast right through till June? Jody paid for his first bike selling apples on the state road. This is the first year Bancroft apples won't be bagged and busheled for Millbrook Grocery."

"Drew, you and your brothers could have eaten them."

"Don't own 'em. You do. Ever seen an orchard torn up? They might take a chain saw to them, then acid in the roots. Or maybe just bulldoze the whole strip, flatten it right out to make room for the condo foundations."

"Stop it. You're being melodramatic and very unfair." She looked at his wrist, inches from her temple as he leaned against the tree.

"Of course I'm not being fair. This isn't a fair fight." He looked into her wide eyes. "Before I'm through you'll see it and smell it and blister your hands with the work of running it, city mouse. I want you to fall into bed exhausted from the effort, and exhausted from fighting us." His voice dropped to a whisper under the canopy of turning apple leaves. "I can't make you love it but I can make you see the love that went into it."

"You throw that word around a lot, Drew."

He tilted his head, his eyes never leaving hers. "It's what makes the sweat and the pain worthwhile."

"You're so damn sure about everything." Holly's voice was breathless as she tried to slow her pulse but all it did was race as she watched his eyes close and his hair catch the light. "You're going to kiss me, aren't you!"

He smiled. "Yes," he murmured. The pressure was soft, the antithesis of his earlier words, as if there had never been any anger in him. He was full of seduction as sweet and tart as the apple that fell with a *plunk* into the grass at his feet.

Holly tried to concentrate on the tree. She pushed back, feeling the scratchy bark at the base of her spine, the stub of a pruned branch between her shoulder blades, a knot at the back of her head. From crown to bottom she was pressed against wood, but from forehead to thighs she was pressed against Drew, and every inch of the front of her was tingling.

He separated her from the bark, worked his left hand around her back and opened his right against her cheek. His fingers were cold over the heat of her face as she whispered, "Drew," but she could feel the rest of him respond to the intimacy.

Her hands moved into his hair for balance as they played a game with no rules. She slid her arms inside his jacket, around his ribs, thrilling to the response, laughing lightly for no reason except that it felt good to laugh. She tried not to think about how he looked in nothing but pajama bottoms as wool and flannel, denim and down set up delicious friction.

He laughed back. "'Woman is fickle, like a feather in the wind...'"

Holly put her hands along the sides of his face, as flushed and warm as hers. "*Not* always changing her mind, Drew. You can't always get what you want."

He brushed back her hair. "So far it has been a pleasure trying."

Five

Holly walked with him back to the house through the arrows of the setting sunlight. She carried apples in both hands, surprised at how hard she had to squeeze them to keep her hands from trembling.

"It was only a kiss," she said as he put his arm across her shoulder.

"I'll try to remind myself of that" was his reply.

The house was dark and Holly made a face as Drew went directly to the wall switch. "You'll learn your way around in time," he said, "or is that what you're afraid of?"

"Dinner smells ready" was her reply.

She gave in to Drew's request and they ate by candlelight, but Holly lit four on the table and six more on the buffet. "I think you missed the point," he said.

"I think I'm avoiding the point," she replied, raising a forkful of duck. "It's delicious. Do you have much time to stalk these poor things?"

"Not much now. I'll get out for geese in November."

"The rest of you, too?"

Drew shrugged. "Some, mostly Kevin and Ryan."

"I suppose Peter taught you. Did he hunt?"

Drew looked surprised. "Haven't you seen the pictures of him with the dogs and the one with the Canada goose? They're right in the folder with the others."

Holly could feel his gaze as she chewed. "I left them where I thought you'd be sure to find them, in the top drawer of the dresser. You are using the room downstairs?"

Before she could answer, he got to his feet and headed for the front bedroom. She followed, saw the light go on and heard the drawer slide open. She got to the doorway as he was opening and closing the rest of the empty bureau. The manila folder had been slapped onto the foot of the bed.

Drew looked at her and then turned his attention to her open suitcase and the neat stacks of clothes in it. "This is your idea of unpacking?"

"I haven't had time," she said defensively.

He shook his head. "I'm not good at lying and neither are you. It shows across your face along with every other emotion."

"Drew, that's enough."

"I know when you're frightened, when you're angry, when you want to be kissed," he continued.

She spun away from him but he took her arm. "You haven't unpacked because of the fear that you might want to stay. You might get to know this house and the man who owned it. You're afraid you might come to understand the time and effort he put into this and into us. You're as scared of loving it as I am of losing it. Sooner or later you'll have to justify the difference between what he was and what you made him out to be, Holly.'' He shook his head. ''I had no idea you couldn't even bring yourself to unpack your suitcase.''

He dropped his hand but she didn't leave. ''Did it ever occur to you,'' she asked, ''that seeing all this care and devotion only makes it worse, only intensifies the anger?''

''You mean the hurt, don't you?'' he asked.

She changed the subject. ''Have any of you considered what I want? That selling this makes *my* goals possible. What I want out of my life may be as significant as what all of you want out of yours. Peter put no stipulations on his estate because it simply went to his closest living relative. Who else was there?'' Who else, indeed, she thought, looking at one of six people closer to him than she had ever been.

Holly turned and went back to the table. Drew was slow to follow, but when he did he carried the folder, which he put, unopened, between them. She had finished her duck before either of them spoke again.

''What do you want, Holly?'' he said finally.

She put down her fork. ''The means to manage my life. There's no one for me to lean on, you know. I was an Italian Studies major. So far that's meant two years in a Renaissance gallery in Rittenhouse Square and six years teaching English as a second language.''

''Doesn't knock your socks off, huh?''

She fought a smile. ''I'm very serious, Drew.''

''Believe me, *mariposa*, so am I.''

"That's it!" she cried. "You do think I'm a butter-fly, doing this on some whim or vendetta. My job's been terminated, thanks to government cutbacks, and I'm unemployed. I've also gotten accepted at the University of Pennsylvania and Uncle Peter's property will make that a reality."

"Many times over," Drew added. "An Ivy League degree and an independent income and you'll be the catch of the century."

Her eyes flashed. "I didn't have a family business to fall into, you know, and I'm not anybody's catch."

"Scusi."

"Your Italian is awful," she replied.

"So's your explanation. You may be Peter Bancroft's only blood relative, but you were also John Bancroft's heir. Surely *his* estate would float your tuition."

"This may come as a surprise to you, but I'm not going to discuss my father's financial situation. It doesn't have any bearing on what I plan to do with his brother's estate."

"That much I believe."

She looked disgusted. "Buy me out, if you're so opposed. It's going to the highest bidder and I don't care whether that's Branigan Cranberries or a Boston developer." She stood up and took their plates into the kitchen while Drew followed with the glasses. "One of you could set up housekeeping here. You love it, why not? Go find yourself a woman crazy enough to put up with all of you. It's certainly big enough for a family."

Drew looked amused. "You mean a bride wouldn't be happy living with a few brothers-in-law and a couple of dogs down the hill?"

"Getting involved with a Branigan is torture enough. Starting married life in that dormitory you call home would be more than any woman could take."

"Are you getting involved with a Branigan?" he asked, still amused.

Holly scraped the dishes and rinsed them. "No more than I have to." She moved suddenly as Drew stepped next to her.

He sighed. "There you go, jumping again. All I was going to do was rinse the wineglasses."

She pressed her lips together. Men didn't make her flinch. They didn't make her do much of anything. She was quite used to small dinners and walks at sundown; an occasional romance was as close as she'd come to losing her heart to anybody. She looked at Drew as they stood side by side and tried to figure out how the conversation had moved from bitter to friendly to frankly flirtatious. Being in the presence of Drew Branigan was like having an inner ear disorder; she could never quite keep her balance.

He touched the barrette holding her hair off her temple. "Are you finishing college or is this graduate school?"

"M.B.A." she answered.

"My, my. I thought for a minute you might have flunked out—too much carrying on."

She looked disgusted and concentrated on swiping the counter with a sponge. "I don't carry on."

"Put the sponge down, Holly."

She kept wiping.

"Look at me," Drew continued softly.

She did, but only after he moved her chin around with his hand. "You've dropped in on us from a pretty fancy address. BMW in the driveway, silk blouses, and your country clothes look like you just cut the tags off. Italian operas and sophisticated aperitifs make strong first impressions. Unless this is pretense and you've sadly overextended your life-style, I don't buy finances as a motive for anything, not even tuition."

"Then why don't you stop buying motives and buy this property! Make us all happy, Drew."

He glowered. "Thirty thousand for each bog acre, fifty for the rest, about one hundred and forty for the house...sorry, kid, I'm a little short."

She stared at him. "I don't understand why Peter didn't do more for you. How can you keep telling me how wonderful he was, how much he loved you? He pulled this right out from under you!"

Drew watched her. "He knew how much he loved you."

Holly recoiled until her back hit the stove. "You're insane."

"Knowing you were loved and never forgotten shouldn't hurt. You've dropped into my life kicking and screaming, throwing up a dust screen for us and I'm sure for yourself, as well. Don't tell me you don't carry on. You've disrupted my life, ruined my sleep and kicked my dogs."

"I did not kick your dogs," she muttered, grateful, as always, for the humor.

"You came close. I want the motive for your behavior, Holly Bancroft." He finished by moving his fingers to her cheek.

She cleared her throat. "This isn't a murder mystery."

"It may be very shortly."

Beneath his touch, her skin glowed and she did the only thing she could think of to keep him off balance.

She put her arms up around his neck and kissed him. She hoped it would work to her advantage, but rational thought oozed out of her. The kiss in the orchard had sparked something that was kindling, and she thought about how to douse her desire now, not his prying. Her intellect melted into puddles of physical sensations. He felt warm as she held him and his sudden intake of breath, the movement of his arms around her ignited everything she fought to control.

The two of them stood in Peter Bancroft's kitchen and kissed as if there were nothing on either mind except the pleasure they gave to each other.

"I like the way you change the subject," he whispered when he had the breath to talk.

"I thought you were going to rinse the glasses," she replied.

He looked at them. "My hands aren't steady enough at the moment."

The phone rang on the counter next to them and Holly's "Hello?" was still breathless. She handed Drew the receiver. "It's Kevin, for you."

Drew said "Hello" and listened. "I came over for the duck I gave her and a little heavy breathing." He was smiling, as usual. "Okay," he finished. "Five minutes."

He put the receiver back as she hissed, "Drew Branigan!"

"You did throw your arms around me, didn't you?" he asked, leaning against the counter.

"Kevin will get the wrong impression," she said.

He watched her. "Heaven forbid he should think you might enjoy my company." The smile stretched into a grin. "That's what you were doing, wasn't it—enjoying my company?"

"Never mind what I was doing. I don't want you to get the wrong impression, either."

"Which impression is that, city mouse? That you're capable of responding to your baser instincts? That you find me incredibly sexy and irresistible or that kissing me until all I can think about is what's wrapped around me might make me forget how close we were getting to motives?"

Her lips parted and her eyes widened. "Lord," he sighed, "you can be the picture of innocence, even when you've got the six of us by the throats."

"I don't."

"Well, there's no time to hash this out, anyway. I've got to go monitor the sprinkler systems. Frost warnings have been called and we'll have to spray the bogs tonight."

"You'll be up all night?"

He shrugged. "Delicate system, takes watching. Been known to put two hundred miles on the truck before dawn just driving from one to the other."

"You and Kevin?"

"Mostly. The others work around their jobs—Ryan and Sean, that is. Jody and Matt are out of most all of it now. Tonight'll just be Kevin and me. And you," he added suddenly.

"Me? Don't be ridiculous!"

"I'm never ridiculous. Get out of that outfit and into something warm. There's a lot more of your education waiting."

"I couldn't care less about sprinkling a bog."

"Precisely why I'm dragging you along. Get some heavy socks over those painted toes and something more substantial than those silly slippers you skip around in."

"Flats to you, and there's nothing wrong with the way I dress." She was sorry she said it as Drew lowered his lashes and his green eyes fell to her open collar and into the neckline. The peaks of her breasts were still a hardened outline against the sheer fabric over them.

Her fingers fluttered over the flush from where her heart still pounded. "Nothing at all wrong with the way you dress," he repeated. "Except the condition you're in is from those baser instincts. You won't feel quite so warm and comfortable when that gooseflesh is from the cold."

She looked at the color across his cheeks. "I suppose you've perfected the ability to blush so you can get away with comments like that. Talk about the picture of innocence!"

He closed his eyes and pulled her to his chest. "Holly... God, how I want to touch you, to make love to you. Almost as much as I want to shake some sense into you. And since you're resisting all of those, I'm going to settle for shaking some knowledge into you instead. I want it all; I want you to understand what you hold."

What she held at the moment was Drew, which she let go of. "You can be very persuasive. Isn't that what you told your brother? As handsome and charming as somebody's fantasy with a technique I'm sure you perfected before you got out of puberty. My baser instincts," she continued with a rueful smile, "react the way any woman's would, but don't mistake it for anything more than simple passion."

"Simple passion? I'll buy that. Somebody's fantasy? You think so?"

She got huffy. "I'm thirty years old and if I want to kiss someone in an apple orchard I will. My innocent eyes are wide open and I'm too old to be seduced, so you can stop thinking sex will make any difference."

"Is that what I've been thinking?"

She pushed him away. "You've had the duck and the heavy breathing."

"What makes you think you're too old to be seduced? You have no idea how romantic it can be in the cab of a truck under a full moon with a dog in your lap and one of us on either side of you." He picked up the phone and tapped out a number.

"Kevin?" he said. "Holly's coming along for the education. Pick us up here. She insists on a first-hand look at the operation."

"What did he say?" she asked when the phone was down.

"Something close to 'my Aunt Fannie,' but it was anatomical." He put a hand on each of his hips. "Now then, I can carry you kicking and screaming into the bedroom and dress you myself or you can do it. In about ten seconds you won't have any choice, and in about three minutes there'll be another one to lend a hand."

"You are an arrogant clod and crazy to boot if you think Kevin wants any part of my being out there with him tonight."

Drew nudged her in the direction of the bedroom. "You threaten what he's worked for all his life. If dragging you around tonight makes a modicum of difference in your attitude he'll keep you out till dawn and charm the pants off you, to boot . . . in a manner of speaking."

"Really," she replied. "I thought he was leaving that to you."

Drew laughed at her, kissed her unsuspecting lips and hoisted her into his arms. By the time she mustered enough fight to make the walk difficult for him, they were in the bedroom where he dropped her on the bed.

"You are also too old to behave like a child, a spoiled one at that." While he spoke, he rifled through her open suitcase and neatly stacked clothes. He turned back with a heavy sweater, turtleneck, socks and gumshoes. "Very good," he said, dropping the footgear on her. "Excellent choice for this kind of work."

He bent again and came up with a bra. "You'll probably be more comfortable in this so you don't jiggle."

She yanked it from him. "I don't jiggle and get your hands off my underwear!"

His smile was ingratiating. "Believe me, when you behave like this, the last thing on my mind is putting my hands on your underwear." He left the room with the door open and she could hear him clearing the rest of the table while she undressed.

"Remind me of that the next time we're alone," she yelled. "And I'm not a spoiled child."

He appeared at the door and she clutched the bra to her camisole. "Spoiled woman," he said. "Very much a woman. I'm encouraged that you think we'll be alone again."

She threw a gumshoe at him.

Twenty minutes later she was back on the front seat of the Bronco. There was no dog in her lap but a Branigan sat on either side of her. A CB crackled for company and she had the honor of holding a thermos of coffee and more muffins.

Kevin maneuvered the four-wheel-drive vehicle along the gravel edging of the dike. She watched the moonlight play on the flooded bog they'd been harvesting that morning. In the night air she could just make out the masses of hulls piled where the elevator had lifted the berries from the water.

Over the whine of the engine, Kevin pointed to the fat, yellow moon pushing its way through the pines. "Painfully romantic," Drew said, reaching into her lap for a muffin.

"Painfully," she answered.

Kevin stopped the truck and opened his door. "If you care to cut the repartee, we can get to work." He motioned for her to follow and the three of them walked along the dike to the pump house at the edge of the pond, which served as the reservoir system. A flick of the switch had started the sprinklers in the flat, rectangular areas not yet flooded for picking. Holly stood quietly in the moonlight watching her frosty breath and the fine spray as the brothers worked.

Her reluctance was being chipped away, not by her escorts, but by her own curiosity. In the moments that followed she asked few but intelligent questions. Kevin's answers were detailed and pleasant. His expertise was evident and there was none of the sarcasm of their earlier encounters.

Drew walked in his heavy boots to a dry sprinkler head, examining it with a hand-held flashlight. "Faulty heads," Kevin said to her. "The system's overloaded and old. It was state of the art in the sixties . . . the last project my father put in before he died."

Holly nodded. "He and your mother were in a car accident?" she asked, frowning at some distant memory. Maybe the news had come on a rare note from Peter or maybe it had been some long-suppressed explanation from her mother. She couldn't remember how she knew, only that her uncle had become surrogate father to the suddenly orphaned boys in Millbrook. It was one of her parents' excuses for Peter's disappearance from her life.

Kevin bent over the piping. She didn't offer sympathy and he didn't seem to want it. He simply said, "Yes, a car accident," and went on with his inspections. "This shoots sixty-five gallons per minute per acre," he said, "but she's straining like crazy under the load."

"So what do you need to do, replace the pump?" Holly asked.

Kevin nodded and stood up. "That and the pipes, too. They're all rusting."

Drew clomped back from the dark, shaking his head. "Shot," he said to his older brother.

Kevin swore and looked at Holly. "This spring we'll modify the whole system. New frost control heads here, pump house in the middle of the bogs, one for the setup on the state road."

She rubbed her gloved hands together. "Would an updated sprinkler system have saved Peter's crop?"

"Most likely," Kevin said. "Can't ever be completely sure."

"You're carrying the loss? Sixty thousand dollars?" she asked.

"You got it. Ten per acre this season."

The three of them got back into the Bronco, and Kevin drove them out past the house, along the main entrance. As they left the silent streets of Millbrook, they talked cranberries, the benefits of lateral piping, the saddle system of lifting the sprinklers above the vines. That is, Kevin and Drew talked. Holly listened, fascinated as her exhausted mind focused on their calculations and assessment of weather conditions. By the time they reached the second set of bogs, she was looking forward to the blast of cold air to keep her alert.

The design was similar, with the bogs, a dike and small reservoir laid out over five acres. They walked her to the pump house. She watched the spray and listened to the soft *whoosh* of the system as the men checked the pump.

They left her again while she ran in place and hugged herself against the cold. After a chilly five minutes, Drew came back to her and pulled a watch cap from his pocket.

"Put this on your head. Heat loss goes right through that gorgeous head of hair. How are your fingers?"

She pulled it on and raised her hands. "Numb."

He smiled and tucked the loose hair up under the wool for her. "Gotta be tough to grow cranberries, kid. Builds character, though, jumping around in the cold, going without sleep."

She shook her newly warmed head at him. "I don't suppose there's anything I can do?"

He smiled down at her, covered in moon shadows. "You could admit that you're enjoying yourself."

She blew a smoky puff of air at him. "Enjoying is not the operative word here."

"Maybe not, but you've been very pleasant, intelligent, interested company—much to Kevin's amazement—and if you're not enjoying yourself, you're putting up a good front. The defenses have been down and I'll bet you've learned a thing or two."

"Perhaps," she answered through chattering teeth.

"Get in the truck," he added softly. "Run the engine for a minute or two with the window cracked. We won't be much longer. Once it's unclogged we'll drive around the whole operation and you'll stay warm.''

"If I'm not out of line, Drew, I'd like to know if this really seems as run-down as you make it appear and if so, why haven't you stayed on top of it?''

"Maybe business does suit you more than Italian culture. No, it's not as run-down as it appears, it's just a system that needs constant monitoring. It's fragile when the weather's hard and you've got to remember you're dealing with a crop growing in peat and sand— grainy stuff, tiny leaves, debris that can make a mess of engines and nozzles. It responds well under constant attention. Kind·of like a woman.''

"What!''

He laughed at her. "Just thought I'd get your circulation going, put a little color in your cheeks.''

She made a face. "Never mind the color in my cheeks. You're facing a major expense, then, after the harvest.''

He nodded. "The loan from Peter took care of all the heavy equipment; water reel's new, elevator's overhauled, flatbed's been added. This is the year we do the sprinklers.''

"Watching you tonight makes me think you've nearly waited too long.''

"Priorities, Holly. Sean built a house and we're putting two of us through graduate school. Ever educate a doctor?''

She looked at him for a moment. "You're quite a family.''

He tilted his head. "Peter Bancroft made us believe we could do it.''

She saw the kiss coming and welcomed it. Two cold faces nuzzled for a second and then lips parted. In the dark her shivering lessened as his tongue traced hers. Drew Branigan was a hot toddy on a frosty night, and she stood, gloved hands at his temples, aching for the rest of him.

"Honest to God, Drew, you can warm her up later" came from Kevin at the edge of the dike.

"I wish the bogs were as easy to warm up as she is," Drew replied so both of them could hear.

She pushed one gloved fist into his down jacket. "What does Kevin think is going on?"

Drew walked her to the Bronco. "What *is* going on?"

"Nothing," she said.

"Everything. Life as Holly Bancroft knew it no longer exists. Not for her, not for us. You leave tomorrow, city mouse, it'll still stay with you. This work, this pleasure is already part of you. You don't need me to tell you that. When you manage to clear away the cobwebs that have been spun around you, you won't be left with a Renaissance gallery in Rittenhouse Square. Sit up on that hill tomorrow by yourself and think about emotional intensity."

"Really, Drew." She opened the door and climbed into the front seat.

"I mean it. Life's been pretty cut and dried for you, I'd guess. Lot of pain, maybe, loss, frustration. You're due for some highs, kid. Couple of sunsets, apple picking, cold air and a man as charming and handsome as a fantasy."

She groaned. "I'm sorry I ever said that."

He reached in and tucked a tendril of hair into her cap. "Upwardly mobile types in Philadelphia don't find

women dressed like little lumberjacks as irresistible as
we do. All those layers of cotton and wool . . ."

She pushed his shoulder. "Get back to your brother
before he blames me for this diversion, too."

Six

Drew laughed and then they were quiet as he drove along the road back through Millbrook and out to their lane. Kevin had stayed behind to tend the sprinklers. As Drew swung onto the driveway, Holly found her voice. "I mean it. It was very generous of all of you to let me stay the other night."

"But?"

She sighed. It was one thing to crawl into a Branigan bed thinking they were all a bunch of mule-headed backwoodsmen. When she'd been covered with plaster dust and ashes, full of fight and determination, Holly hadn't given a thought to much more than their obstinacy and her miserable circumstances. But that was before.

Before Drew had started kissing her senseless... Before I enjoyed kissing him back, she thought, opening the window a crack to sharpen her wits. At the fork of their shared driveway, Drew idled the engine.

She looked at him, enjoying the blast of frigid air coming in. She wasn't sure how it had happened, but in less than twenty-four hours he had stripped away most of her resistance to everything as easily as he pulled loose plaster from her hair. She didn't want to think about Kevin as someone intelligent and business oriented, or Ryan and Sean working two jobs to educate their brothers. She preferred a blur of impersonal hostility.

"I'm fine over here," she said finally. "You all were very generous last night, but that was an emergency. Everything's in order now. The workmen will be here in a few hours, anyway."

"You shouldn't be alone. We have plenty of room."

How she loved his face! She looked at it now, illuminated by the porch light she'd left on and the moon that had hung over them for hours. She hoped to find some arrogance there, or conceit. Presumption would have given her something to fight against. There was nothing but concern.

"I've been alone since college, Drew. I'm comfortable, really. Until the arrangements for Peter's house are settled and I go home, I expect to stay there. By myself," she added.

When he put his hand along her cheek she closed her eyes and leaned against it. "That's the difference, I guess," he said. "I've never been alone. It's been kids and dogs, guardians and DSS workers as long as I can remember."

"DSS?"

"Department of Social Services. My grandmother tried to keep us together at first. She owned your property and sold it to Peter."

"She's the Branigan on the deed?"

He nodded. "After my grandfather died, she moved to an apartment in Plymouth and when my parents were in the accident, she moved back in with us. Six boys from five to seventeen nearly did her in. Peter had worked for us, had a place of his own going and when he realized it was either split us up among relatives or foster homes, he convinced her and DSS he could take over.

"It made a man out of Kevin but he never had time to be a teenager. I guess one of us had to be sober and responsible. Ryan and I were terrible, testing everybody and everything. I was crazy with anger; didn't want anything to do with Peter, and the more he helped the worse I got."

Holly gave him a smile. "Obviously there was a turning point."

Drew studied her and Holly's heart jumped. It wasn't the first time she realized Drew had funneled the conversation down to her own situation.

"He knew about grief, Holly, and how a kid can disguise it as anger. He knew about losing people he loved, about starting over, about life . . . about loving life even when it kicks you in the teeth."

"Drew, it's very, very late and I'm exhausted. You'll have to finish your story another time."

"He knew about people who coat their emotions with layers of polish, the way they lacquer their nails, and how destructive it is."

Holly slid to the door and yanked it open. "Don't trouble yourself over my emotions; they've done noth-

ing but get in the way." She stamped over her driveway, grinding the peagravel under the gum-soled shoes.
When she heard Drew get out she kept up the march,
watching short puffs of her breath shoot into the night
as she approached the dark house.

He caught up to her at the tangle of bittersweet and
holly where she'd watched the fire. "Get rid of the
cobwebs. Admit to yourself that that's why you're
here."

She looked back at him. "I'm here to settle an estate
and get on with my life. There's no sense denying the
emotional tangles we seem to weave, but they won't af-
fect my judgment, especially immature garbage dredged
up from my childhood."

"It's garbage heaped over real emotions. You were
the pawn of three selfish adults, but when mistakes are
made, they can't be taken back. Holly, no one can erase
what has already happened. All you can do is just what
seems the least painful or the most healing."

"Peter mismanaged my father's investment through
deceit and dishonesty. They severed all their ties and he
moved up here for a fresh start. I understand that,
Drew, do you? My father, John Bancroft, climbed back
up, just like his brother. Every hour that I'm here I have
to remind myself of this. Emotions have nothing to do
with it and neither do the hurts of a child left in the
middle."

She stood in the moonlight and looked at him with
eyes glittery from brimming tears. He took a step forward but she raised her hand. "Please don't. I'm too
tired to think and I'm too tired to fight. Drew, lots of
families have feuds. I lead a lovely, uncomplicated life.
Peter Bancroft didn't love me? Okay, that is not the end
of the world, not even a very big trauma, especially

compared to the tragedies in yours. But six months ago
Millbrook attorneys told me that I'd inherited everything he owned, right down to a loan to you and Kevin.
Everything! My parents are gone, Drew—there's no one
to give me answers."

"You hold the answers as much as you hold the
questions. Slow down and you'll see that."

Holly shook her head. "You wrap me in cobwebs,
just like everybody else."

Drew reached out and touched the tree next to them.
"How about if I tell you these holly trees are here for
you? You were never forgotten, never replaced." He
laughed. "Certainly not by six wild boys knocked apart
by tragedy. You wouldn't have been replaced by fifty of
us. It's just that we gave Peter the stability he needed to
make his own life worth something. We grew up hearing about the niece and the business collapse, and then
he planted holly in the front yard to remind him of what
he'd left behind."

She pulled a shiny leaf off its stem. Her head ached;
she was cold and tired beyond reason. When Drew
pulled the cap off her tumbling hair, she still stood
stiffly in his arms.

"Don't sleep alone tonight," he said. "There's room
with us, any way you want it."

She stared at the holly. "No, Drew. My brain fuzzes
over when I get within ten feet of you. I'll never make
sense of any of this with you and your brothers bad-
gering me. I need to be alone." She could feel his reluctance.

"All right, but I'll leave the kitchen door unlocked.
Let yourself in if you change your mind. Holly?"

She finally looked up into his eyes, melting at the
undisguised look of desire in his face. "Yes?"

"Childish emotions are often the purest and simplest and truest ones of all, not that I couldn't love a woman whose brain fuzzes over now and then."

"Go back to your bogs, Drew."

"Good night, Holly."

He stayed just long enough to see her in and turn on a lamp. She closed the door, went to the kitchen for a glass of milk and glanced at the manila folder of photographs still on the dining room table. It stayed there while she dressed for bed, folded her clothes and stacked them back in the open suitcase. At two minutes before 3:00 a.m. she went back into the dining room, picked up the folder and carried it into the bedroom.

Ridiculous! What was she afraid of? First thing in the morning she'd give them a look. Holly fell asleep calculating the expenses her neighbors were planning for, and reviewing the explanation of frost control. If nothing else, this crazy way to make a living was a challenge.

Less than four hours later she was up and dressed to greet the carpenters, the masons and the chimney sweep who inspected the damage, climbed on the roof and agreed to come back and give it a thorough cleaning when the work was finished.

The realtor was waiting for her call, one she decided to make when the patching was finished. Holly went out on the farmer's porch with a cup of coffee. Down the hill the flooded bog danced with fractured sunlight kicking off the water. Men were thigh deep corraling the berries with their wooden booms. On the far side of the dike one of the Branigans stood on the water reel beating the water as the machine churned its way over the submerged vines. Holly squinted but it was impossible to tell one brother from the other at that distance. There were four of them out there three of whom, she knew, had gotten no sleep. She watched the machinery and chided herself for worrying over what was obviously their autumn routine.

When she turned her back, it was to look at her own bogs, berryless but crimson, nonetheless. The color gave the illusion of success. Like us, she thought. This was the property she would walk with the developer, the view someone would pay handsomely for. With her mug of coffee, she took off for the orchard, striding through the dew-damp blades of grass with her heavy gumshoes until she reached the first apple tree, the one where Drew had kissed her. She touched the bark, letting the raised wood rub against her palm. Overhead a flock of geese honked as their V broke in the wind and re-formed above the pines.

There was none of the crisp, frigid air of the night before. The temperature was already in the sixties, warm days and cold nights, which made the foliage brilliant. Holly shaded her eyes with her hand while she watched the Canada geese, and when they were gone she marched back up the hill to rinse out her mug.

Ten minutes later she was outside again with the remnants of the box of trash bags used by the fire fighters. Peter's storage barn, oddly neat now and newer than the house by seventy years, still held his lawn tractor. A few garden tools hung on the wall, and bushel baskets were stacked in the corner. What harvesting equipment he had owned was the Branigans' now; the only major piece of equipment Holly had to dispose of was a late model GMC pickup truck and plow that took up the right bay. She looked at the mower and the truck and the red plastic gasoline containers. What a city girl didn't know about running them, she was about to teach herself.

She put the bushel baskets into the back of the truck, grabbed man-sized work gloves from the hook and got into the cab. Automatic drive, she thought—a piece of cake. The truck lurched backward out of the building where Holly made a Y-turn and eased it down the cart path to the orchard. She was running on a thermos of coffee and a tankful of determination. After mastering the tailgate, she got down to the task of picking the apples.

The task was backbreaking, but by four o'clock she had filled the truck with bags of discards and debris and two bushels of edible fruit. It was a sane place to stop but with two hours of daylight left, she traded the truck for the mower. It, too, had an automatic ignition, and once she got it started she managed to bump her way through the clutch and gears, engaged the blades and began to slice her way around the tree trunks.

She rode to the far end of the neatly spaced trees and turned it around. Drew Branigan, arms across his chest, leaned against the first trunk. She could feel his eyes on her as she worked her way toward him. As she approached, he finished a MacIntosh and threw the core into the bog.

"I had no idea you'd take my instructions to heart!" he yelled over the engine.

"I have a realtor coming, land to sell!" she yelled back, ignoring her heart and its incessant pounding.

"Of course," he called back, grinning. "How stupid of me. You didn't do a bad job for a city slicker. Has it occurred to you that this time tomorrow you won't be able to move? You've spent the whole day using muscles you didn't know you had. No sleep, either."

"Never mind about my muscles." She looked at him with the same late afternoon light shining on him as when he'd kissed her at the tree twenty-four hours earlier. He seemed interested in doing it again. She recognized the look and hoped her own expression wasn't as transparent.

Up at the house a horn sounded from the carpenter's van, and Holly turned off the mower. They yelled they'd return in the morning, and she waved them off. In a normal voice she asked Drew about trash removal.

He laughed. "This is Millbrook. You have to haul your own garbage. But if it's clippings and rotten apples you're worried about, we'll take them for compost."

"Where?"

"Next to the barn. Want to drive me home?"

Holly's smile was shyer than she wanted it to be. Small as the encroachment had been, Drew had managed to expose a layer of emotions tightly capped, a lifetime of questions never answered. He instilled trust where she hardly dared to look for it and as she drove the mower back to the barn she reminded herself that this was the man whom she heard convincing his brother of his persuasive techniques.

She wanted to talk to him about all she had accomplished, about the sprinkler system she'd analyzed while she mowed. Had he seen the migrating geese? Did he notice the way light broke when wind rippled the flooded bogs? Talk from tender places would only give him the wrong impression—that she was changing her mind or regretting her decision. After these few days together, Holly was already able to anticipate his response. She refused to think about what that implied.

Instead she concentrated on parking the mower and hanging the tools.

He waited at the entrance to the building while she finished. "In," she said, pointing to the truck.

"Want me to drive?"

She scoffed. "Automatic transmission. There's nothing to it. You macho types have us all fooled. This thing even has power steering. I'll bet I could plow when the snow comes." She turned on the engine and eased it into reverse. There was one deep rush of emotion when she realized what she'd implied.

"Forget I said that," she mumbled. She could feel the easy smile.

"Not on your life. You can do anything you set your mind to, plowing included."

Good, she thought. He'd missed the slip.

"And that includes considering life in Millbrook. That's what's terrifying."

Her turmoil increased. He hadn't missed the slip at all. She cleared her throat. "Scared of me, huh?"

"Concerned about what you can do without even realizing it. Your naïveté is as terrifying as its consequences. One way or another I'm going to make you see that."

She dropped the gearshift into forward and steered past her uncle's house, out the drive and down the Branigans' lane. The silence wasn't comfortable, but neither of them spoke until she had eased the truck down the hill. Lights were coming on in his kitchen. She imagined them all around the wood stove, eating whatever it was bachelors ate, throwing scraps to the savage animals at their feet as they drank and swore at one another.

It was a lot less heart tugging than patterns she had already glimpsed: gingerbread, good strong coffee, clean sheets and honest concern. Partnerships, bonds, goals...love... She hit the brake, sending Drew lurching against his seat belt.

"Put it in park," he said. "I'll back it up to the compost."

Still silent, she put her hand on the door handle. He touched her shoulder. "There's plenty of room, Holly. Slide under me."

She looked disgusted. "I don't trust you one inch in here."

He tugged her playfully toward him, anyway. "We've got more like six, I think." When she was free of the steering wheel, he raised his hips. She scurried over the seat to the passenger side.

"Drew, let go."

"Look at me, please."

"I'd rather get the clippings dumped." She brought her eyes up to his.

"This is real terror, isn't it?"

"Drew, I'm not scared of you."

"That's not what I mean and you know it. You're frightened of your own feelings. The ones underneath the I-mean-business-let's-get-this-over-with act. The ones that make you soft and human. Doubt is human."

"You conceited clod!"

"I would have said perceptive. Perceptive enough to see the confusion tearing you apart. You admitted last night that you can't understand why your reaction to this is so emotional. As an adult, you find it irrational to feel so strongly about someone who wasn't a parent or a sibling. A child doesn't measure the loss in rational terms. You loved him; he left you.''

"I didn't! I don't even remember him.''

"No one wanted you to remember him.'' Before she could protest, he put his open hand over her breast. She could feel the warmth through the flannel as she brought her cold fingers over his.

"You're fighting yourself in here harder than you're fighting the six of us put together.''

"If there's some crazy chemistry between us, it can't get in the way. The rest of you I can deal with, but, Drew, there's been enough hurt in both our lives. Starting some silly little affair because we're attracted to each other, knowing it can't go anywhere, would only make things worse.''

"And what if there's pleasure for both of us? The pain is from locking life out.''

She managed a small smile. "You don't strike me as someone who's locked much of life out.''

"Ah, everyone's fantasy?''

Her smile deepened. "You always know when to back off, don't you?''

"Perceptive,'' he repeated.

He stopped talking and maneuvered the truck around to the neatly fenced garden. A touch of frost had wilted what hadn't been tilled under, with the exception of a neat row of brussels sprouts and squash vines.

She tried to concentrate on the garden and not the responses that made her feel turned inside out. It wasn't his face, or the blush, or the green, observant eyes. It was the way he manipulated every fiber of her with easy confidence and genuine concern. She didn't want Drew's generous spirit. Couldn't he see he was walking on nails? Didn't he know how much this could hurt?

He turned off the engine and smiled at her.

"I want you to stop caring about me," she said. "I want you to treat me the way your brothers do."

He snapped his fingers and waited. "Gee, kid, I don't seem to be able to." Instead he took the sides of her face in his hands and kissed her, playfully, gently, deeply when she didn't resist. "I have a promise to keep," he whispered.

She ignored the hint as she tried to ignore them all, but when every fiber of her was screaming to trust him, to let Drew Branigan clear the cobwebs, the fight dissipated. Her own hands went around him and she could feel contentment settle into him. She was lost in the way it felt, in the still new game, in the thrill.

His fingers moved over her shirt as hers went into his hair. She felt the brush on the buttons and moaned when he traced the laced edge of her bra.

"Drew—"

"You may not believe this, but I've never made love on the front seat of a truck," he murmured. "Ryan tried it years ago."

"And you could if you had to?"

His hand stayed against her while his thumb massaged the softness under the lace. "Holly Bancroft, I could make love to you anyplace, anytime."

"That's what I'm afraid of."

"Don't ever be afraid of that. I want you . . . I want us." He laughed raggedly. "Though I think I'm past the front-seat-of-a-truck stage." He pulled his hand away slowly and made a design in the glass. "It's been a long time since I fogged up a windshield."

She was about to give him a smart reply but he turned back to her and buttoned her open shirt. She closed her eyes again and savored it. "I wish you were a C.P.A. in Philadelphia or an M.B.A. in Wilmington."

He chuckled. "Doctor, lawyer, Indian chief?"

"Anything but this, Drew. Anything."

Seven

They got out of the truck in the dusky light and heaved the bagged clippings and apples into the boxed compost. "Waste not, want not," Drew said, folding up the plastic bags.

Holly found it hard to be witty. "The apples in the baskets are for you and your brothers, if they'll take them."

He arched his eyebrows. "Generous."

"They're rotting. Better you than the deer and field mice."

"Of course. We can't have the wildlife destroying what the hungry bulldozers will be chewing shortly. I'll make it a fair trade," he added as he stooped into the vines and pulled a jackknife from his pocket.

Holly took a giant step backward as Drew stood up, hoisting a healthy orange pumpkin onto the tailgate.

"If I get a minute, I'll come over and we can carve one hell of a jack-o'-lantern. Maybe that'll persuade you to stick around till Halloween. Sean's kids..." His voice dropped and the end of the sentence was lost to her.

She had closed her eyes, her fingers pressed against the furrow between them. "Thank you. I've got to get back now," she said.

"Holly—"

She backed up and put her free hand on the edge of the truck. "Really, I want to get back to the house."

"Christ, you look like you've seen a ghost. It's the pumpkin, isn't it? I know about it. I know the last thing you did with Peter was carve a pumpkin."

"You've always known and I didn't remember until this week? What did he do, discuss his former life with all of you when he wasn't spouting librettos?" She yanked open the door of the cab as Drew stepped toward her.

"He told me about the pumpkin, one fall afternoon when he showed me the holly bushes." He followed her into the truck. "Move over. I'm taking you home."

"I don't want you to take me home!"

"When has that ever stopped me? Give me the keys." They were in the ignition still and the instant she reached for them, Drew turned on the engine. "This is no time to go into your Greta Garbo routine."

"But I want to be alone, Drew."

"So you can stick your head in the sand? Sorry, darling."

He brought the truck around the bend from the garden to the barn and along the gravel toward the house. The patch of lawn in front of the kitchen was a blur of bodies, dogs, discarded waders and heavy boots. A

towheaded toddler was in Sean's arms and another had
Domino in a bear hug. A good portion of the activity
stopped as Drew eased the truck to a crawl and parked.

"Come on in for a minute," Drew urged.

"I don't think so."

"They don't bite, Holly."

"They'd like to."

While the engine idled, Drew got out. Holly was surprised to see Matt and Jody, who dutifully went to the
back of the truck when they were told about the apples. Drew stooped to pick up his niece, gently separating her from the Lab's collar. Kevin came to the truck
window as Holly slid behind the wheel.

"I brought you some apples," she said for lack of
anything clever to open the conversation. She could feel
the flush that still remained on her face, as much from
kissing Drew as from arguing with him. "I didn't want
them to go to waste."

"Thanks. I'll see one of us makes you a pie in return," Kevin replied.

She looked at the fatigue in his face. "Don't be silly.
You're all too busy..."

He put his hand on her shoulder. "I was kidding."

Holly said, "Oh," and from behind Kevin, Ryan
called that the bed was still available. She wanted to
throw out quips the way they did, but she ached with the
effort of holding back her turmoil. Their animosity had
frustrated her but it had given her a solid wall of emotion to stay behind. Gentle teasing and good-natured
hospitality had no place in her scheme of things.

Behind Kevin, Matt told Drew he was leaving for his
shift at the hospital. Orders were being given as they
both turned to look at the bogs. Holly watched Drew as

he absentmindedly stroked the curls of the toddler who
had buried her face in his shoulder.

"Stay for dinner?" Kevin asked, making Holly shake
her head.

"No, but I want Drew to stay here." Kevin gave her
a studied look and nodded.

Drew came back to the truck still carrying his niece.
"This is Kate, first girl in three generations. In four
years, I don't think her feet have touched the ground for
more than five minutes."

"Hello, Kate," Holly said. She looked at Drew and
the child, and then Sean with the second daughter.
Identical twins whose lives were no longer parallel, she
thought, glancing at the unbanded finger on Drew's left
hand. Had it just been a few short days before that she
couldn't tell the men apart?

Drew handed Kate to Kevin, but Holly shook her
head. "No. Stay there. You're exhausted; you've got
work to do. I want to be by myself." She didn't need to
look at him to know he wasn't buying any of it, so she
dropped the transmission into forward gear and drove
up the hill. In the side mirror she saw Kevin yank his
arm. "Let her go" drifted over the crunch of the tires.

By the time she'd made herself a hamburger and
salad, every muscle was complaining. Apple picking
after three hours sleep had taken its physical toll; holding back unwelcome memories and confusing emotions capped the soreness with a splitting headache.

She ran a steaming tub of water after admiring the
repairs begun around the fireplace. Fresh wallboard
sealed the hole, the joint tapes sealed and drying. The
bricks had been repointed, the hearth cleaned with acid.

The room was clean, the furniture straightened; it
made the catastrophe lose its impact. It seemed proof

to Holly that with logic and without panicking, any situation could be resolved. She snapped off the lights in the parlor, grudgingly admitting that Drew Branigan had been instrumental in the repairs. She wouldn't have gotten this far if he hadn't stepped in. *Interfered*, she thought, even though he knew delays would be in his own best interest, not hers.

By seven o'clock the hilltop farmhouse was dark, with the exception of Peter Bancroft's bedroom and adjoining bath. Holly piled her hair up, using half a dozen barrettes and combs, and lowered the rest of herself into the hot water. It undulated over her. She looked at her polished toes and thought about the flooded bogs. Then she thought about the six men down the hill.

Sean would be home now, back in his new house with his girls. She thought about Matt driving back to school and the rest of them sitting around the stove. She tried not to think about the double bed in the front room upstairs.

Alone in her unwanted house, Holly closed her eyes and pushed away the memory of Drew arranging her covers and how close they'd come in the cab of the truck—too close. Under the warm clear water her breasts rose and fell as she relived his touch. No one saw the pulse pound under her jaw or the flutter of her hand as she caught her breath. The water lapped and she closed her eyes again. He seemed always about to smile or about to kiss her, about to spin her in a web or clear it. She didn't know which was worse.

Drew and Kate, uncle and niece, looking out at the day's work, blond head, darker one, safe, contented, holding back the rest of the world... All those years Peter Bancroft had remembered carving the pumpkin.

At first Holly didn't make a sound. She leaned her
head back on the porcelain rim of the ancient bathtub
and let tears flow over her cheeks. One followed the
other along the bridge of her nose and into the corners
of her mouth. Her breath caught in her throat, and she
choked on a sob until she finally let go. She cried, feeling ridiculous pangs over memories she had obviously
sentimentalized, and after splashing her face with water, she washed her hair and got out.

She rushed through the rest of the evening ritual,
dried her hair and pulled on a flannel nightgown. Falling asleep wasn't quite as simple, but she managed, and
by eight o'clock the whole house was still.

Seven hours later she was wide-awake. She lay still for
a minute until she was sure nothing external had broken her sleep, but the house was quiet.

It was a windless night, more frost warnings. She
thought about the Branigans monitoring their bogs as
the sprinklers misted their crop. After five minutes of
mind wandering, she snapped on the lights from bedroom to kitchen where she poured herself a Scotch.

She had meant to make herself relax, but the liquor
went down like fire, radiating through her whole system. It was then, with the drink and her insomnia, that
she picked up the manila folder from the bureau.

She got back into bed, left on a single lamp and let a
lifetime of her uncle's mementos spill onto the quilt.
There were Branigans everywhere, children, teenagers,
school photos and Sean's wedding...identical twins and
their four brothers with a woman who must have been
their grandmother. The hunting picture Drew had
mentioned was there: Peter and Kevin, grouse laid out
at their feet. There was one of Drew and Sean holding

ducks. She recognized them all, knew the backgrounds now and the distant buildings.

The last of the bunch was Peter atop a water reel, slapping cranberries to the surface on a day like the one just passed. The resemblance to John Bancroft was strong, and though she tried not to, she stared at all of them, absorbed everything. There was nothing in any of the shots to indicate that this man with the shock of gray hair would have known anything of the turmoil he'd left in his wake or that he held any memories, good or bad, of a previous life.

Holly looked at the wallpaper. Her hatred of the orphans down the hill was a childhood fantasy, one devised to make Peter's loss bearable. She was an adult now, and it was time to come to terms with it. She pushed the lot back into the file and took out the second envelope.

Her features knitted into confusion and her hands began to tremble. Many were sepia toned or black and white; they were all of Bancrofts. Peter, John and their parents at a New Jersey beach, a jumble of ancestors, the bogs amid the truck farms of the Garden State. Her mother was in half a dozen, including one as a bride. She looked young, younger than Holly now, in a long white gown with her arms draped around John, the groom, and Peter, the best man.

The shock was what was left. More than half were of Holly. She blinked hard against tears and took the last swallow of the fiery drink. Holly in front of a Christmas tree, at a birthday table, in a class play, dressed for a prom. The chronological order ended with the senior picture taken for her yearbook. It wasn't flattering and she shuffled through the pile, sure she'd find the one she'd had taken six months later.

Maria Bancroft had died during her daughter's last year in high school. Holly had arranged to have a portrait of herself made as a Christmas present to her father the following December. It had given him the emotional boost she had hoped. Dozens of copies had been ordered and sent in his Christmas card, none apparently to his estranged brother.

In fact, Peter Bancroft's collection ended with that traumatic year when Maria died and Holly went off to college to study Italian in honor of her mother's heritage.

Holly pressed the elastic wristband of her sleeve over her eyes. Even alone, she was overwhelmed by the ache and confusion. She got out of bed and went back to the kitchen, rinsing the liquor glass under the tap long after it was clean. Crying this long was bound to be cathartic, but she stood at the sink feeling nothing but upheaval.

In front of her on the panes of the kitchen window, there was a light tap, making her start so violently that she shattered the glass against the faucet. She turned the water off and stood still, listening to Drew's knocking and the muffled "Holly, let me in."

"I don't want you, I don't want a duck, I don't want a kiss. It's three o'clock in the morning. Go away. You have no business scaring the life out of me by tapping on my window." She would have been more effective if she hadn't been sucking in hiccuppy breaths and fighting for composure that wouldn't come.

Drew came around to the back door and stepped in as the cold air rushed around Holly's thin flannel. She closed the door behind him. "Go home."

"I missed you, too. You're lit up like a Christmas tree over here. I just wanted to make sure there wasn't a problem with the house. From the look on your face the problem is not external."

She gave her nose a swipe with her sleeve. "Save your middle-of-the-night concern for your sprinkler system." She looked down at his thick, heavy boots.

"I've just finished with the sprinklers. What is it?"

"Nothing. You don't know anything about women— you said so yourself. We like to have a good cry once in a while. Unmolested, in private, behind closed doors, and if you'll just go back to your own house—" Drew turned from her and started through the dining room. "I mean it!" she cried, trotting after him, kicking at her hem.

He didn't stop until he reached the doorframe of the bedroom where he looked at the glossy display on the bed covers and back to Holly. She was careful to keep her distance. His arms came out to her.

She backed into the foyer. "Don't do that."

He opened his arm slowly. "Don't do what?"

"Don't look all concerned and sad and then smile that smile."

He smiled the smile. "Holly, please—"

She took another backward step, catching her heel in the flannel. "Don't touch me, Drew. I'm not dressed for touching."

She watched the softness creep over his face. Damn, how she loved his face, and how the ache moved around inside her. She put her open palms out. "Don't come any closer."

He opened his hands, working slow, warm circles over hers. "Talk to me, darling. Tell me about the pictures."

"No!"

He spread his fingers and curled them in between
hers, pulling her forward so fast that she wound up flat
against him. He still had on a down parka and she
didn't feel anything but the soft *whoosh* of the ripstop
nylon as she pressed into it. "Talk, damn it."

"I can't. You're mashing my face into your chest."

"Feels good, doesn't it?"

She wriggled. "Never mind how it feels. There's
nothing to talk about. I couldn't sleep, so I finally took
a look at the pictures you gathered. I was surprised,
that's all, to find ones of me."

"That's good for starters."

"Well, it'll have to do for finishers, too," she replied. "I'm going back to bed." She was relieved that
the tears had drained her grief—if that's what it was.
Her equilibrium was shaky, but returning.

He let her go. "Get into bed. I'll turn out the lights
for you." Drew turned and started for the kitchen, and
it seemed safest to move in the opposite direction, so she
went back into the bedroom. He came in as she was
scooping the photographs back into their envelope.

Holly lifted her head, tucking a piece of hair behind
her ear. The rest of the house was dark behind Drew. He
stood framed by the single light in the room. There was
tension in his mouth, concern in his green eyes and a
flush across his cheeks.

She looked at him without turning away. From the
first moment, they had communicated without words.
Simpatico, she thought.

"We watched you grow up," he said so softly that she
could barely hear him. She sat down. "Through these
pictures Peter kept. They sat with ours on mantels, and
tables and in his wallet. I left them here thinking you'd
want them, assuming you'd looked at them the first

night. When I discovered you hadn't, I realized you still didn't know." He took her by the shoulders, but held her at arm's length.

"You won't break apart. You're tougher than you know. We grew up around you, in a way. The last pictures were when you were seventeen or eighteen."

"All this time...no one ever mentioned it." She looked at the darkened window as she sat on the bed. "Where are the rest of your brothers? Did they send you over here?"

He shook his head. "No one sends me anywhere. I just saw the lights on my way home."

"They were teasing me this afternoon," she added.

"They don't know what the hell to do with you. It isn't often that one little city mouse can disrupt the lives of six hulking men."

She almost smiled. "Me?"

"You, kid. When you were just a glossy face it was easy for them to want to tear you limb from limb. *Over your dead body* came damned close to everyone's sentiment when those orange property markers went up. There's fear in all of us, Holly, that you'll destroy—"

"Don't use that word! I have no intention of destroying anything."

"Land development is a Pandora's box. You have the power to change the real estate base in this corner of the county. There's a twenty-thousand dollar difference in the price of an acre of buildable land and the price of an acre of bog. How many growers will sit by in a bad year and fight that? Sell a bog for thirty when they can fill it and sell it for fifty? A little simple math will tell you the temptation to get rid of a couple of acres here and there and before you know it, you can't afford *not* to sell."

"Peter's is just a small parcel, Drew."

"It's big enough. Holly, you're making us crazy. You impressed the hell out of Kevin last night with your analysis, your interest in the sprinklers, even your silly determination to stay awake. It's as if you're offering a little glimmer of hope where you keep swearing there isn't any. Six grown men aren't used to fighting something cut and dried on paper, which turns out to be all blond tangles and sweet blue eyes in person." He sat down next to her, still in his parka and boots. "You don't exist in a vacuum. You touch lives and you touch hearts, whether you mean to or not."

"I don't mean to," she said stiffly.

"And lives and hearts touch yours. Life is supposed to work that way, but I think in your case, it's happened so late you have to give yourself time to digest it. And digesting it alone isn't going to do you a bit of good."

She looked at him dry eyed, but trembling. "Drew, you and I are no good, either. I don't know any other way to say it. In the end there would just be more pain." She could feel the pulse in her neck, the steady rhythm that hadn't lessened since he'd knocked on the window. "You are a constant reminder," she whispered.

"Of everything you're afraid to face?"

"My pictures stopped when my mother died, didn't they?" Her question was rhetorical. She didn't want answers from the Branigans, especially this one who sat looking into her soul with eyes darkened by desire. Without shifting his weight, Drew unzipped his jacket.

Maybe for a little while she wouldn't have to think. The parka went on the floor next to the boots, and once he was out of them he moved up on the mattress, facing her. "You *are* dressed for touching," he murmured. It made the grief and the anger and confusion dissolve.

Her hands shook as she worked the buttons on his chamois shirt, more so when he brushed one last tear across her cheek. When she finished and the shirt lay on the floor next to the parka, he put his head on the pillow. Holly lowered her head and kissed the tip of his breastbone, steadying her hands by feeling the rise and fall of his chest, still rhythmic and smooth. He snapped off the light, lowered her back next to him and got up. She watched as he raised every shade, flooding the room with high, bright moonlight. He stepped out of the rest of his clothes.

"Are you protected, Holly?"

Oh God. "For what you're asking, yes, Drew."

He kissed her forehead. "You've spent most of your life protecting yourself from everything else." He worked the buttons at her throat and moved his hand over one breast and then the other. "You are beautiful in this light. You look the way you did on the bogs."

"I had three layers of clothes on under that moon."

"I know. I kept wishing you didn't."

She moaned as his head moved still playfully over the fullness. "I don't suppose you'd like to talk now, would you, Drew?"

"About us?" he asked.

"There isn't any *us*."

"There has always been us, Holly. There always will be. You've been part of my life for twenty years. Sit up for me." She did and he eased the nightgown over her head, weaving his fingers through strands of her hair when she was free. She loved the gesture, especially when the caress continued down her bare back.

"We're not children anymore," he continued. "You and I have some control over fate. You're at a fork in the road, city mouse."

They knelt on the crumpled sheets at the cool end of a long night. Drew brushed her hair over her shoulder blades. She shook it into place by arching her back. His fingers cascaded from the hair along her spine and around to the tip of her breasts, already tight and aching. She wanted to call him, but he said her name first in a gasp of delight.

A shaft of moonlight from behind her moved across his chest as she watched him catch his breath. Her eyes followed the light down over the rough hair and its dark trail. I can make him happy, she thought. This one night I can give him that.

When his hands left her breasts, he looked into her eyes and then lowered his lashes and his face. The agony of wanting him began to simmer, settling under every surface that his mouth and fingers touched. She could barely move.

"What will your family think?" she gasped as they fell into the pillows.

Drew took a deep breath and finger-walked her ribs. "We lead independent lives, you know. They're asleep. Millbrook's asleep. The whole world's asleep as far as we're concerned, Holly." His smile was dream inducing. "Where was I?"

"At my right breast," she murmured.

"Victory," he whispered but the hand cradling her tightened, pressing her to his chest. Even humor was getting to be a problem.

She kissed his ear. "For someone unaccustomed to the rituals of women, you seem to know your way around," she whispered back.

"I've had a little practice . . . so I could be perfect for you." He moved to her other breast and she still watched, mesmerized by the planes and surfaces of his body and the hunger she was able to build.

"Has there been love?" she asked.

He slowed and looked at her. "I've come close a few times, but nothing that's knocked my socks off."

Holly smiled at his familiar expression, but when he asked her the same question she gave him the same answer. He looked at their feet. "We seem to be sockless at the moment. Must be love."

"Couldn't be" came too quickly.

He was quiet, his hands still. "Why does that scare you so badly—love in any form?"

"It doesn't."

He stayed silent, but she didn't elaborate. "If you're not going to expound on that point, I'd like to get back to this one." His mouth found the nipple again and she responded by swaying against him. "God, you're beautiful. Let this be beautiful, Holly. Let me show you."

Compliments came so easily to him. They warmed her the way his touch did, swept her along his path even with her heels dug in. The flannel and down was long gone and so, for the moment, was every obstacle she had managed to erect between them.

Eight

Holly clung to him, feeling the heat rising from her breasts over her throat to the pulse points. She began to knead the muscles in Drew's shoulders until he raised his head. The cool air played havoc with the moist spots left by his mouth, and she shuddered.

She lifted her hand but he covered it with his own, guiding it down along the two of them as he looked into her open face. "It's all right, tonight's perfect. We're perfect." His voice was husky, his eyes closed, and she pressed her cheek against his roughened jaw.

Perfect for the moment, she thought. I'll make it perfect for you...for the moment. He was ahead of her, far ahead, she hoped. Even the sound of his rapid breathing deepened her desire and loosened her control. He moved his hand away but hers remained, the fire built and blazing. This was what she had planned, what she wanted, a moment's satisfaction, an episode

totally enjoyed for the moment it was. It was all there
had ever been. But there had never been Drew.

With one arm he brought her against the undulating
motion of his body. The tender tips of her breasts
scraped against his chest, her cheek against his jaw. She
pulled away from the erotic friction, concentrating on
Drew's pleasure. The more she gave to him the less
likely she was to slip away where emotion was too raw
and honest.

"It's perfect now," she whispered, but the more she
touched him and denied what she couldn't admit, the
closer she came to the edge. One step back would have
been enough, one pause in a thundering heartbeat. Her
eyes were wide, clouded with desire, and she turned her
head.

"For you, too," he moaned, setting the pace her
body raced to follow, her mind fought to control. No
beat was skipped as he moved against her and tensed,
the fever peaked.

It was all she'd wanted, all she'd anticipated, but she
was shimmering in her own fever as she watched the
hard desire in his moonlit face soften into rapture.
"Holly," he whispered, kissing her temple and her
mouth during the slow, sweet decline.

She thought she'd go mad with fighting it, prayed
he'd been too oblivious to notice. Drew's breathing
steadied but his heart continued to pump against her.
He smiled that deep, devilish Branigan smile and
brought his face back down to hers, his mouth at her
ear. "Come on, city mouse," he whispered.

There wasn't any resistance left in her, and the moment she relaxed under him he moved again. "Drew!"
she gasped as glittery light broke behind her eyes, shat-

tering the fever into splinters of heat. She buried her face in the crook of his shoulder.

"Take what's yours," he whispered, holding her until she was still, pulling the quilt over them after a long, silent moment. They held each other in the dark, and he played with her damp hair.

"There's enough fight in you to beat back an army, love. Don't turn it on yourself. I wish you wouldn't turn it on any of us, either."

She started to speak, but he pressed two fingers over her lips. "Let's not spoil what we've had. Not tonight when we've come so far," he sighed.

"Too far."

"Not nearly far enough." He kissed her again.

"This will only get in the way of what has to be done."

He looked at her without responding and then pulled himself out of bed. The thrill of watching him dress made her heart jump, but her pulse had slowed. Her breathing was even and part of her recoiled at the intimacy he must now assume would continue.

He bent over her as he zipped his jeans. A trickle of perspiration caught the light on his breastbone. "Sleep a little more. I'm going down the hill to my own bed before they miss me."

She smiled. "A gentleman."

He dressed, worked his socks into the boots and started for the door.

"Drew?"

He waited and, when she didn't continue, came back to the edge of the bed, picking up her nightgown from the pool of moonlight. "You can ask."

"Stop reading my thoughts," she stammered.

"God, how I wish I could." He sat down next to her with the gown between them until she pulled it over her head.

"Do you know...was it my mother who sent the pictures to Peter? Was it an excuse to keep up the relationship, to try and heal the rift between my father and Peter?"

Drew buttoned her bodice, looking at his fingers. "The pictures came from your mother, yes. Peter never made a secret of it in those days. It was just news from home, to us. Pictures of his niece."

"I don't think she ever told my father. She was crying the day Peter left, when we carved the pumpkin. I think Peter was, too." She stopped, overcome suddenly with exhaustion. It was nearly dawn.

Drew brought his head up, his features as drawn and sleepy as hers. "Do you understand that no matter how you feel, no matter what you do with this, you can trust me? You don't have to go through this alone."

Holly's eyes moistened, but she simply nodded.

"You're not a child who can be manipulated anymore. It won't hurt to think about what you're starting to remember. Peter loved this and he loved you. He never manipulated you in life and he wouldn't in death. It was his dream that you'd come up here and see what he'd done with his life, but he would never have stipulated that you couldn't use it to your own advantage."

"Even if it meant the wrath of the Branigans?"

Drew smiled and got back to his feet. "He knew we'd never go down without a fight. I think this is exactly what he had in mind."

She didn't see any of the Branigans until midway through the following day. The berries in the flooded bog had been trucked to the cooperative processing plant in Middleboro and the rest were still on dry vines. She hoped her neighbors had the luxury of waiting while they caught up on their sleep.

Ryan's car was gone, so maybe he'd patched things with Johanna, Holly noted. Sean was probably at the fire station. It disturbed her that she thought of them as individuals and speculated on their lives. She found herself wondering if medicine came easily to Matt and if Jody studied law with Kevin's determination and Drew's insight.

As tired as she was, Holly let the carpenters back in and finished giving the orchard a little polish. She was stiff and sore, and she winced as she tossed a handful of apples into the ditch lining her uncle's berryless bogs.

Twenty acres of buildable, desirable land, surveyed and ready to unload...Holly winced again, this time at her mental choice of words. She wasn't unloading it. She was ensuring a comfortable future for herself. Even Drew had softened when he admitted that Peter wouldn't have put any stipulations on the will prohibiting her from doing what she wanted...what she thought best.

The problem now was that she wasn't one hundred percent sure she knew what was best. What in heaven's name had made her go to bed with Drew! She threw one last apple into the vines as slivers of an all too recognizable feeling worked their way through her. So what! She was a thirty-year-old woman entitled to simple physical attraction. Half of Millbrook was probably panting after him.

Abruptly she squinted into the sun and turned back to do the chores at the house. Where had rationalizing gotten her? What was the point in keeping him at arm's length when the unmistakable chemistry had tugged at her since he'd stuck that duck in the door? She looked up at the house and shielded her eyes. Soon it would be over, anyway, and she'd be settled and sane back on Spruce Street in Philadelphia. And rich, Drew would have added. Holly frowned at the intrusion and put her hand against her stomach, willing herself not to think about how he'd looked in nothing but moonlight.

Holly's designer jeans were now work pants, smeared with lawnmower grease and traces of apple. By the time she got up to the holly and bittersweet, she had added garden soil and a coffee stain. Her hair was braided, one on each shoulder to keep it from falling into her eyes as she trimmed the orange berried vines to make door wreaths. The picture of country life, she thought, as she paused next to the holly. One shiny, green point punctured her finger and she sucked the droplet of blood.

Maria Bancroft had tried to heal the rift between her husband and his brother right up until her death, a noble, unsuccessful effort. The sudden intrusion worked its way through Holly's consciousness, pushing everything else aside. She hadn't intended to think about her mother.

The pictures of the only child must have been the excuse for occasional letters and updates written to Peter. Had Maria never mentioned it to her daughter for fear of John Bancroft's reaction? Holly stood in the afternoon sun and thought about her parents' civil relationship. *Civil* seemed an odd, but appropriate choice of words.

Behind her, the sound of an approaching vehicle made her turn and a beam of sunlight glinted off the windshield of the Bronco. At the fork in the shared driveway, it idled. She wished she could put her heart back in neutral as easily. She brushed her hands on her denimed thighs and the braids off her shoulders as she walked to the driver's side. Drew was at the wheel, his twin in the passenger seat. Kevin and Ryan sat in the back, every one of them in business suits or sports jackets and ties. She looked once around the blur of oxford cloth, navy wool and silk ties, then back to Drew. Her fingers self-consciously worked a braid tip. She felt like Heidi on a bad day.

"You all look dressed for Rittenhouse Square."

"Been to the bank, actually." Drew was looking at her as though he was recalling the way he'd seen her last.

"Oh. Financing the new sprinkler system?" she asked.

"Partly," Kevin said from the backseat, his window down.

"Did they do all right last night?"

"Drew saw to that. He took the shift at the pump house till dawn."

She patted Drew's elbow, which rested on the window frame. Two spots of color were already staining his cheekbones. "Devotion," she replied with a smile. The man was incapable of deceit. What a time he must have had as a troublesome teenager.

With his back to his brothers, he looked at her and said, "Devotion."

"We could use you tonight if the warnings come in," Kevin said lightly, teasing.

Oh, no you don't, she thought. There were enough webs around her already. "I have to get ready for the realtor and then I'm going home" came too quickly. The men looked surprised. "The repairs will be finished this afternoon. Peter's insurance is taking care of the bills . . . the rest should be wrapped up, as well.''

And this infantile crush on your brother, she thought, finally lifting her hand from Drew's arm. "I can't stay any longer. I never intended to.''

"Things don't always turn out the way you intended, no matter how strong the fight in you," Drew said, looking her straight in the eye. Everything began to slip. Holly busied herself with the bundle of bittersweet. "Place looks nice; hasn't had a woman's touch since my grandmother gave it up," Drew continued.

"Sold it," Holly said, willing herself not to flush for any of a number of causes. "Sold it for her own reasons, for her own gain." There was a hesitation between them, just short of awkward. "Don't let me keep you," she said with false brightness. She stepped back from the Bronco. How did she appear to them? Confident? Master of her fate? Someone not to be toyed with?

The car rumbled down the hill. A Dutch boy holding back the Hoover Dam was closer to the truth.

The carpenter had left; the chimney sweep was due in the morning. Nothing remained but the cleaning and inspection. She would wait for the realtor's advice on matching the new wallboard. A fresh coat of paint and removal of all the wallpaper would freshen the parlor and cheer up the house. Someone would fall in love with its coziness and antique detail. Holly envisioned it as an appendage of the rest of the units that would eventually grace the property. Bittersweet Hill or Bittersweet Acres? Perhaps she'd have a say in what they'd call the project.

Holly was tacking her bittersweet wreath to the front door when Drew came across the lawn. He was back in the casual clothes she was used to, the sunlight streaking his hair with copper. There was no mischief in the Celtic features, no spring to his deliberate strides. She left the wreath on its hook, came down from tiptoe and wiped her hands self-consciously on her jeans. He had nearly reached her when she realized he wasn't going to stop.

"Drew, what are you doing?" she cried, backing up, pushing halfheartedly against his sweater with open palms.

He hugged the breath out of her and then kissed her, which she returned like a schoolgirl. When she pulled back, he took a braid in each hand and tugged her forward. "Kiss me like you mean it. Do what you did last night and then stand there and tell me you're going back to Philadelphia."

She looked at him and watched him smother his hurt with sarcasm. "I've always been a sucker for dirty jeans and braided hair," he murmured, kissing her until she responded.

"It's broad daylight" was all she managed before she kissed him back as though she meant it. His hands went under her cotton jersey, touching the places, repeating the movements that had brought the deepest response the night before. There was no way on earth she was going to do the same.

"You need a cold shower, you Irish madman," she gasped, rocking back on her heels.

His green eyes were molten. He rubbed his hair and took deep, ragged breaths. "I need you in a shower; you're the one who drives me mad. You can't be serious about locking this up so soon."

"You knew my schedule." She couldn't look at him.

"I thought last night might have extended it."

She swallowed. "Last night was nothing more than what it was."

"Look at me and say that."

That brought her eyes up. She hated the perceptiveness she always saw in his. Through the anger, through the desire, it was always there. "What happened between us can't change anything. You know that as well as I do. Snow job or no snow job."

"This is a snow job?"

Her complexion deepened. "The attraction just happened. That's all. I'm very flattered, but I don't for one minute think I'm any different from any of the other women in your life except that getting me into bed . . . you thought that might change my mind about all this." She raised a limp hand and waved it vaguely.

When he didn't reply, she took a step away from him and focused on the distant hills. His hand pressed her shoulder and she turned back, anticipating anguish in his face.

"You were in an awful hurry to make me happy, city mouse."

Her eyes widened; she fought the blush.

"I seem to have struck a nerve," he continued. No anguish, no pain. He looked close to self-righteous.

"You haven't struck anything. I'm just not used to such intimate conversation. Drew, you're making me very uncomfortable."

"Good. I have every intention of keeping you uncomfortable. Is there someone in Philadelphia?"

"No. I told you that last night. What kind of a person do you think I am?" She regretted it the minute she'd said it.

Drew smiled. "I think your greatest fear is that I might find out. You're a full-grown woman, indepen-

dent and self-sufficient. A woman who thought she was
fully prepared for Millbrook, fully protected for last
night.''

"Could we please talk about something else?"

"A woman of modesty and reserve, who shyly offers
to provide pleasure—"

"Damn it, stop this." She tried to leave, but he put
hands on both shoulders.

"—as a smoke screen. No man caught up in that
much—what shall I call it, Holly, fun?—would notice
Holly Bancroft's teeth-clenching determination to feel
nothing but a few fireworks before she got back to
reality. What kind of a woman do I think you are? One
embarrassed down to her painted toenails, not by the
intimacy of what I've just said, but by the truth of it.''

Her pupils danced over his smug expression. "You
conceited, egocentric fool. I'm sure it comes as a shock
to any Branigan, but you are just a man, Drew. Growing up in a fraternity house with the wonderful Peter
Bancroft as parent did nothing for your perception, no
matter what you think you know about my relationships with men.''

When Drew spoke again, it was a whisper, nearly lost
in the breeze that blew his heavy hair across his forehead. "My perception comes from my relationships
with women, Holly. From years of wanting nothing
more than what I've just described. A little bit of fun,
not many regrets . . . This is the eighties—the women in
my life haven't wanted any more than that, either.''

"You're contradicting yourself."

"Our relationship isn't built on a little fun; it's built
on my desire to keep you from making rash decisions
out of anger. If you leave here tomorrow, you'll still
have to face the questions. The lid's off the box. That's

why you came. Nobody in Philadelphia's going to help you face the answers. You're pushing everything into fast forward because there aren't any more barriers between us.''

She walked away from him, her back to the sun, casting one long, ill-proportioned shadow over the autumn grass. ''And because you've been thinking about Maria all day,'' he finished in a voice that carried to her. He had pronounced her mother's name *Mar-ee-ah*, the way the family had, with a familiarity that made the hair on the back of her neck rise. Something knotted in her stomach.

Holly stopped and turned around, her arms dead weight at her side. Drew was already next to her, leading her to the farmer's porch, where he sat on the step and patted the boards next to him. Holly joined him.

''Did Peter talk about my mother a lot?''

''No, to be honest.''

''I feel like I'm in a fishbowl,'' she sighed.

''What he did say wasn't to all of us, either.''

She looked at him. ''I think I sensed that all along. Were you closer to him than the rest?''

Drew gave her a shrug. ''I was more trouble than the rest. He put more energy into me because he had to. The rest of them cried and grieved the way they were supposed to. I picked fights, broke windows and skipped school. Peter wouldn't let me get away with it. He made me pick a project and work it out through exhaustion until I returned to the human race.''

Instinctively she touched his arm. ''What did you pick?''

Drew's jaw flexed. ''It was my idea to put in the orchard.''

The silence between them seemed interminable. "Did it bother Peter that my mother wrote and tried to patch things up between him and his brother? She must have kept using photographs of me as excuses to fire off letters to him. Obviously it never worked. My father never mentioned Peter unless I brought him up. Even that was rare and there certainly wasn't any reunion. Uncle Peter had my graduation picture, so I guess Mom kept it up right till the end."

"Right to the end," Drew repeated. "She wrote when she knew how sick she was."

"Peter had to follow his own advice in dealing with his own loss, then, I suppose, assuming he cared anything at all. You're teaching me what he taught you, aren't you?"

Drew shrugged again. "You're too smart to try to convince yourself that all you want is the means to glide through the rest of your life with an independent income.

"Holly, Peter's death is still raw for all of us. I can't even listen to those foolish opera records yet. The six of us keep expecting him up on the egg beaters . . . or the invitation to come up here for chowder after being out all night with the sprinklers. Compromise, love. Hold the land for a year and then make a decision. There's not a man among us who wouldn't welcome your presence."

"Do you think Millbrook or even Plymouth has anything for an Italian Studies major? What would I do with this ark of a house?"

"Bring it back to life," he said, kissing her. "Do you realize that this is the first time you've declined without ranting and raving and putting up that smoke screen?"

"I don't want to talk about smoke screens." Two more minutes of this would make the ache that was already in her chest move her to tears of worse, passion. She watched Drew look at the wreath on the door. "The bittersweet's for the realtor and so were the repairs. I want the house and the grounds to look as desirable as I can make them. I give you my word that what goes up here won't disturb you and your brothers unless you let it. Life does go on, Drew, and sometimes accepting change is the best way. Sometimes it's the only way."

His eyes darkened but there was no argument. "Give me the rest of the day," he said suddenly.

"For what?"

"I want what's left of the afternoon. I want you to dress, come to the house for a drink and let me take you to dinner. We'll go to the French restaurant in Plymouth I mentioned. I want one honest-to-God date before I have to harvest again or stay out all night with the pumps. Give me that before we're at each other's throat again."

There was no denying the thrill that went through her. "Will you behave yourself?"

"Only if I have to."

"You have to," she said.

"Crumbs," he muttered, "but better than no bread at all."

Nine

Still grubby, she walked him down the hill to his house but declined the offer to enter. Drew went in and emerged moments later, the dogs at his heels. "Kevin wants us here at six. He's going out for dinner later, as well."

"My, my, the impenetrable head of the clan?"

"He can be pleasant company when pressed."

They walked with Domino and Max along the cart path toward the bogs. The wind was strong, rare for late in the day, but a good omen: no frost. "I like your nieces," she said while she threw a stick.

"Sean got lucky. You'll like Annie, too. They were teenage sweethearts."

She moved closer to him, matching his stride. "Maybe if you'd had one you wouldn't have broken so many windows or skipped so much school."

"Who's to say? Maybe I'd be the doctor in the family."

She took his arm. "I can't imagine your doing anything else. You'd never love anything—or anyone—the way you love this."

Drew wove his fingers through hers as they crossed the dike separating the bogs and skirted the pond. When they reached the far side he bent for a stick, sending the dogs scampering into the field grass.

"Falling in love takes as much effort as running a business. What I said at the house is true." Her footsteps faltered and he tightened his fingers. "Don't go turning purple on me, Holly. I was only going to say that we've always been satisfied with things the way they were, not looking for a lot in our relationships. Most of us, that is." The blush was his. "Christ, Holly, you've got me falling all over myself. That's what drives me crazy about you."

"What?"

"Your emotions. You're a combination of modesty, determination and passion, a bundle of contradictions nobody can get hold of. I'm sure that's just the way you want it."

"I don't want any more than what I've already given." She was already defensive.

"A nice choice of words. You have so much to give."

"Is that Sean's house on the other side of the pond?" she asked, looking at the new saltbox colonial.

Drew nodded. "Am I not supposed to notice how deftly you changed the subject?"

"Yes."

The house sat facing the water, the weathered shingles gray, the trim white: neat New England. A wooden swing set sat in the side yard. "Want to go say hello?" Drew asked, "You haven't met Anne."

She shook her head. "I'm having enough trouble with the ones I have met."

Drew put his arms across her shoulder. "You come so close before you pull away."

The dogs were back, tangling with each other as they skirted the water. It gave Holly something to focus on, and she bent to ruffle their fur. "Will each of you build on this property when you have families?"

Drew knelt with her. "It's a possibility for each of us. We really haven't talked about it since there's been no need. I don't think Jody or Matt will wind up here. You never know."

"But the idea of new houses over here is fine. Just don't let me do it."

"Holly, it's hardly the same thing."

"I'm not suggesting that it's the same, just that a good architect might not detract but enhance the value of your property."

He looked at her sideways. "The value of our property for house lots. Look, I asked for one day. I won't talk about sex if you won't talk about property values. There's a long evening ahead and I'm not about to ruin it. Stick to dogs or old movies or something safe."

She thought there were precious few topics safe to discuss with him as he tugged her to the edge of the water. "Now take the pond, for instance—it's the water source for this entire set of bogs." He pointed out the flues and the pump house, all of which were familiar, and then he kissed her.

Holly closed her eyes, savoring the pressure on her mouth and the soft *whoosh* of surprise, and she lost her breath kissing him back. The feel of his tongue tracing her lip was velvet, and they played while the dogs lapped the water.

"That was a surprise," she whispered, catching her breath.

Drew fooled with her braids. "I said I wouldn't *talk* about sex, not that I wouldn't try to engage in it."

"Cute." She pushed him so that he lost his balance and sat down on the weeds. "Keep it light, Branigan."

"You're saved by the clock. There's not enough time left for passion *and* a tour, and right now I want you to see things. Later you can feel things."

"Drew!"

"False modesty," he cried, getting to his feet. "You're not even blushing."

She smiled. "No, but you are."

He led her over the acreage, through the stand of pine and birches that bordered the western side of the property, along to Sean and Anne's home. They went back to the house by way of the barns where the heavy machinery stood ready. Drew looked over her head at the vegetable beds and the flourishing pumpkin patch.

She didn't want him to bring up the subject of pumpkins, so she kept up a conversation about self-sufficiency and putting up tomatoes and the longevity of apples stored in a cool place.

She felt confused by the issues that separated them and the desire that kept bringing them together. "I'd better go back to the house and shower," she said quietly. "I need some time to get ready if this is to be a real date tonight."

"There's no need to rush," Drew replied.

She watched him read her thoughts as he looked from her face to the vegetables. "Peter said he'd always had a pumpkin patch and we should have one, too. We have ever since. We used to have carving parties.''

"I wonder if he ever sent pictures of this to my mother; if he ever responded to her letters with pictures of you and the farm," she said wistfully. "Of course not. I would have known."

Drew began to walk toward the hill. "Go take your shower. I'll be up just before six. Look like a million bucks, Holly. Don't forget half the women in Millbrook would give their eyeteeth to be in your shoes.''

"Oh, yeah? Why don't we take my sneakers with us and we'll see who tries them on,'' she snapped, relieved to have something to joke about. It seemed to relax Drew, as well, and he laughed.

"A million bucks, city mouse.''

She put her hands on her hips. "By the time I leave these sand hills, that's what I'll be worth."

Holly put on *The Barber of Seville*, showered and got her circulation going with stiff terry toweling. She was cold. She was nervous, too. Traipsing around in jeans and braids was one thing; a real date in a real restaurant was another.

When her hair was dry and sweet smelling, she put it up in a ring of tortoiseshell and curled the ends around her fingers. She pulled on a lavender crepe dress over peach underwear and stood at the bathroom mirror while she applied makeup. Maybe he wouldn't recognize her. Maybe he wouldn't want to kiss her and nothing would get started.

Holly bent over the sink and brushed on mascara. She'd be jelly by then. She'd have to say her good-nights in the car.

She feathered blusher over her cheeks, not that she needed it. What if he took her parking? Parking! Adults don't go parking. No, she thought, he thinks they just go home and jump into bed. She took a minute to shake her head and wonder what she'd gotten herself into. She didn't bother to fathom why she fought it so desperately.

Out in the parlor, Dr. Bartolo sang for the thieves to be arrested, and discovered his niece was now a countess. While the doctor forgave Rosina, Holly decided to drive her own car. A BMW might add a certain note to the evening...the Bronco was dirty...she could drive him home.

She put the album away, left the outside light on and pulled her dress coat over her shoulders. Arriving in her own car would show an independent spirit.

Holly pulled the navy blue sedan from the spot where it had sat since her arrival. With the exception of shopping for food, she hadn't ventured beyond where she'd walked today. She drove down the hill and left her car next to the others.

Four man-size pairs of rubberized boots stood at attention on the back stoop. She took it as an omen, bent to greet Max and knocked. Drew opened the door. "I was on my way up," he said.

"I drove," she replied.

"Great!" He smiled. "I've been dying to give it a spin."

Kevin came up behind him. Both men were dressed in gray flannels, polished loafers and blazers. Drew took her coat and whispered, "Two million," as she followed them into the living room. Ryan was on the couch. He got up and shook her hand.

"I thought you'd be out arresting people," she said.

He smoothed his chamois shirt. "Millbrook's in good hands." Holly glanced over her shoulder, expecting another Branigan, and Ryan laughed. "This is all there is," he reassured her.

She shrugged. "You never know over here. Any minute another one might leap from behind a chair."

Kevin stood at the open Governor Winthrop desk, an impromptu bar. "What can I get you?" He handed bourbon on the rocks to his brothers.

She cleared her throat, hand against the flutters. "What do you suggest?"

"A double martini," Drew said. The three men stood waiting for her to sit.

She looked at the pleasant, expectant faces. "Why do I feel like a lamb led to slaughter?"

"Sit down," Ryan said.

"I don't think so," she replied, taking a glass of white wine. "As a matter of fact, I don't drink much, either, so why don't you just tell me what this is all about." She gave Drew a look that would have shriveled most men and he gave her one that would have melted most women.

"Please sit down," Kevin said. He meant it and she did. There were a few preliminaries. Kevin talked about the business, its future and how his father had started it with his grandfather when there were just peat bogs there.

"Peter first arrived as my father's manager," he added.

"Yes. He left us in New Jersey when the business failed. Poor management, I'm surprised your father hired him after—"

"After a year he bought the property he left to you." Kevin cut her off firmly.

"With the money he took from us." She drank the wine. "Did he ever tell you that?" She put her empty glass on the coffee table. "The man you all think deserves sainthood left his estate to the wrong person and none of you can stand it. Peter Bancroft, surrogate parent, had the audacity to leave what had been yours to me. Me, some silly little thing in Pennsylvania, you think, who only wants what she can squeeze out of it."

She sat back in her chair and crossed her legs. Three sets of eyes astutely avoided watching. "It has always looked to me as though he was acting totally in character. Drew's been working overtime trying to convince me of the kind of man you all want me to think Peter was. I see him as the man who nearly ruined my father, went selfishly on his way and continued to ignore even my mother's attempts at reconciliation. I think it's lovely that he propped my pictures around and remembered me in the will. It probably did wonders to soothe the guilt. Why would I want to hold on to anything that reminds me of him?"

Kevin flushed and looked at Drew. "You'd better straighten her out."

Holly got to her feet. "There's been too much of that already. Things are much clearer in the daylight when I'm not within fifty yards of any of you—especially you," she said, looking into the green eyes that hadn't left her face.

Drew joined her and then they were all on their feet. "Holly, the only issue now is the future."

"We want to lease it from you."

She looked at Kevin. "The bogs?"

"All twenty acres."

"It's unproductive land, except the orchard. You know that. Kevin, your emotional attachment is getting in the way of good business sense. What about the sprinkler system? All these bogs and those on the state road...that's a twenty-five-thousand-dollar expense right there. Your judgment isn't very sound.''

"I'll worry about what's sound judgment," Kevin replied. "Think about it for twenty-four hours."

She shook her head as Ryan got up. "Drew, forget the half-baked idea that you could make her listen. Holly, what's it going to hurt to go home and live off what you've already got and Branigan checks? You've got the loan for the equipment already. It's *your* emotional attachment that's in the way. Being a silent partner isn't going to kill you." He looked directly at Drew. "Just how tangled up is she?"

Against her peach camisole, Holly's heart thumped until it hurt. She'd spun her own cobwebs this time. She didn't look at Drew.

"I'm leaving," Ryan added. "My idea of a night off isn't combat with the girl next door. That's your department, Drew. You always were a sucker for those pictures. It's a shame, Holly. You're so damned stubborn you'd fit right in with the rest of us." He moved from the group and went up the staircase.

Kevin was the next to speak. He offered his hand, as cold as hers was, but the handshake was firm. "I want your word that you'll give this twenty-four hours."

"I don't see—"

"Twenty-four hours!"

"All right!"

"Good." He looked at Drew. "Take her to Santé, wine and dine her, whatever it takes." He had the audacity to smile at both of them, but the look he gave to Drew was full of implications she couldn't read. "Make sure a can of worms isn't on the menu."

Holly looked at both of them. "We've already opened one."

"Since you have," Kevin said to Drew, "you'd better think hard about what she needs to know." He mouthed something silently to his brother before he nodded to them and left by the front door. It had looked suspiciously like *tell her*, but when she asked, Drew's reply was to ask for her car keys.

"You don't have the faintest idea where we're going," he said, by way of explanation.

"I want to be in charge," she snapped.

"I've noticed." He put out a flat palm. "You know as much about these roads as you do about Peter Bancroft. Give me the keys, please. I'm not going to kidnap you."

She handed them over. "What's that supposed to mean?"

Drew sighed heavily as they turned off the lane and drove through Millbrook. "It means that he loved you, never stopped loving you or caring about your family."

Holly looked out the window as they approached the village green and its historic district. Handsome, oversized colonial houses lined the east side, facing quaint shops. At the far end the fire station had its wide glass doors open. She recognized Sean's truck in the parking lot.

On the other side of town, Drew turned on her car stereo and pushed a button. "It's set for Philadelphia," she said, finding a local FM station.

He made a face and nodded. The commerce gave way to fields again, wide, dark stretches of bogs and pine picked up in the wash of headlights as they pulled onto a main thoroughfare. On either side, tract housing filled the landscape. Suburban Plymouth, civilization, she thought. They followed Route 44 into its final intersection.

"America's Hometown," Drew said as they pulled north on Court Street.

"It looks like anybody's hometown from here," she remarked. "Where's the water?"

He touched her knee. "After dinner, I'll show you the harbor and the *Mayflower* and the rock and Ocean Spray, if you're lucky."

"How do you always manage to slip cranberries into every conversation?"

Santé turned out to be a renovated Greek Revival house, intimate, sophisticated and understated. There was nothing understated, however, about the way Drew was greeted.

A brunette in a lambs-wool dress was bending over the lady's writing desk, which served as the reservation lectern. Her face lit up as her arms went around his neck. "Drew," she sighed, "I'm so flattered that you picked us for tonight."

Holly's brows knit. "Andrea Carter," Drew was saying, "Holly Bancroft." He didn't offer any more explanation.

The women shook hands cordially. "Welcome to Santé," she said. "Welcome to Millbrook and Plymouth, for that matter. You certainly picked the perfect time of year to come to New England."

"Thank you," Holly replied, skipping the it's-nice-to-be-here refrain. She looked at both of them.

Andrea turned back to Drew. "Come on upstairs. I put you by the front window."

The thick carpet blanketed their footsteps as they went single file to a small, candle-lit table. Drew held the chair for Holly and Andrea handed two menus to him. She whispered something in his ear and then added that their waiter would be there shortly. Her smile was as bright as the Branigans'.

After Drew watched her disappear down the stairs, he lifted his water goblet. "Andi was my first romance."

"Back when you were skipping school and breaking windows?"

"Peter had to convince her parents to let her go out with me."

Holly shook her head. "That bad, huh?"

"She was there through a lot of the bad times, my parents' deaths, Peter's..."

Something tightened in Holly. Why should she care? "That's a span of twenty years," she said quietly.

"I know. She had the nerve to marry David Carter, one of my best friends more than ten years ago. Hard as I tried, I never did get her socks off."

Holly grinned, and the light made rainbows as it filtered through her glass. "Twenty years and her secrets can still make you blush."

"No secret," he said, exploring her face. "She just whispered that you're far more beautiful all grown up than you were in the pictures. And obviously worth the wait," he added after a hesitation.

"Drew, please," she replied, but under the crepe and camisole was the warm, prickly sensation of pleasure.

The four-course dinner was perfectly prepared, perfectly served and quietly eaten. They held the truce and talked about Andi and David, Plymouth, tourists, sailing and wine. There were childhood anecdotes over dinner and the welcome intrusion of the chef over demitasses.

"David!" Drew got up, only to be settled back down.

"I just wanted to come see for myself." Holly offered her hand, which he ignored in favor of a kiss on her cheek. His chef's hat bobbed as he straightened. "Has he gotten you into waders yet? Branigans are always looking for free labor. Watch this guy very closely."

"I am," she laughed. "I have to."

"We're flooding tonight, start picking again tomorrow. Feel free to stop by," Drew said to him.

"Right." David looked at Holly. "Get him to tell you about the year I fell into the truck. All they cared about was how many of the little buggers got smashed." He patted her shoulder. "We're glad you're here. Enjoy the rest of the evening."

She did. It was impossible not to. Drew's spirit infused her with something she might have called happiness if she'd given herself the time to analyze it. Even though it spread over the underlying tension, one perfect night was what it had become.

They left Santé after ten and drove back down Court Street toward the center of town. "Memorial Hall," Drew said, nodding at a brick building on the left. "Next week the Philharmonic's doing an all Beethoven program."

Holly laughed. "How would you know that?"

Drew made a left-hand turn and approached the harbor front. "Because Branigan Cranberries underwrites the October soloist and I sit on the board of directors."

She looked at him as he cut off the engine. "You're not kidding, are you!"

"Because I don't care for opera, I can't support a symphony? Holly, things aren't always what they appear and people aren't always as simply put together as you might want."

Drew got out of the car and came around to her side. "Come for a walk," he said.

She got out reluctantly and stood with her hands in her pockets while the wind whipped her hair loose. Drew buttoned her coat. "Breezy," he murmured. "It'll keep the bogs from freezing, and it'll keep you close to me." He kissed her and tugged her toward the water.

As they walked, she looked at the commercial boats at anchor, draggers and lobster boats ready for their captains at dawn. She and Drew moved along the parking area, under street lamps, past a seafood outlet and up the town wharf. It smelled of fried clams, raw fish and hard work. Once past the parked cars, they had the night to themselves.

"*Mayflower*'s moored right down there," Drew said, pointing east into the dark. "Over at that park. The rock's there, too, and the tourists. This is where the work gets done."

Before she could reply, he cupped her ears against the cold and closed his eyes. Drew tasted of fine French burgundy and strong Brazilian coffee and he kissed her until reason vanished. She was light-headed with the feel of him, soaring in the night air like the gulls they'd disturbed.

At the sound of a door being closed, they parted. The assistant harbormaster zipped his foul-weather jacket as he finished a cup of coffee and threw the paper cup into a receptacle.

Holly cleared her throat as he said, "Eve'n."

Drew returned his greeting. "Somebody overdue?"

"Lobster boat limpin' in. Everybody's safe."

Drew put his arm around Holly. "Not a bad night for a rescue."

The official smiled. "Not a bad night for romance, either." He eased himself onto the dragger moored at the wharf and from there moved into the patrol boat. The VHF marine radio crackled with a call to him, and Drew and Holly began the walk back to the car.

"It's beautiful," she whispered, snuggling into his warmth. "Wonderful food, excellent company, romantic atmosphere. My mother loved seafood—Maryland crab, especially. She would have loved this."

Drew stopped in the shadows between streetlights. He looked at her and took her by the shoulders. "People aren't as simply put together as you might want," he reiterated. "Holly, your mother saw this."

Holly looked at him and frowned. "Plymouth?"

"What you suspect . . . what you can't bring yourself to ask is true."

She tried to move from him, but his grasp tightened. She watched a gull circle above the harbormaster's office and perch on the peak of the roof. "What I suspect? That she tried to reunite the family by writing about me once in a while? Drew, when was my mother here?"

"The last year of her life. When she found out. She came to see Peter, to tell him. She stayed here in town, on the water and came out to the house for dinner."

"She met all of you!"

"Maria met all of us. I think she wanted to make sure Peter was happy," Drew replied.

"That life had gone on for him just as it had for her? There wasn't any try for a reconciliation between the brothers, was there?" Holly asked. Her mind was clearer than it had been for a week. She thought about her uncle's departure, the tears and the pumpkin. "They had an affair. They were lovers. He seduced my mother *and* made a shambles of the business! My God, no wonder he walked out."

Ten

They went back to the car in silence and as Drew drove home, Holly found a classical station on the radio. It gave them even less reason to talk. Silently she worked it all through. In her head she put neat little pieces together until she had given herself neat little explanations.

Millbrook was asleep. Even the Branigan house had few lights in the windows. Drew drove up to Holly's door and turned off the engine. She'd forgotten all about her intention to drive.

"This old house has needed your touch," he said. "There's so much you could do with it."

"Face reality, Drew."

He touched her cheek. "That's been my line all along."

Holly turned from him on the pretext of looking at the house.

The porch light shone through the windshield, illuminating Drew's darkening eyes. Holly looked at him as he brushed his hand over the steering wheel. "I should have known this would be how you'd react. It's what I've been afraid of all along. Peter was a devoted man, a man of conscience and principle who made more sacrifices than your broken heart can imagine."

"My broken heart? You're being ridiculous. He was nothing to me before, less now." Holly opened her door and got out. She marched to the door and then stood stupidly while Drew came up behind her.

"I seem to have the keys," he said, and unlocked the door.

"Thank you." She watched the puff of her breath. "You didn't have to go to all this trouble tonight just to soften the blow."

He smiled. "You know me too well. Never mind, a little royal treatment never hurt. I enjoy impressing you."

"You can be very impressive." She paused and touched his arm.

"Let's go in," he said softly. "I want to make sure you're all right."

"Of course I'm all right," Holly protested. "You didn't expect me to fall apart, sobbing into your arms, did you?"

He ushered her over the doorsill. "That would be too much to hope for."

Once inside the warm house, Holly took off her coat and hung it in the foyer closet. "Would you like a drink?" she asked, aware that this one perfect night was about to end.

"Will you talk?"

"Look, Drew, I'm fine." She walked with him into the kitchen where he got out two glasses and poured them drinks.

"Tell me about school. When does it start?" he asked.

"I could begin as early as the January term or wait until next September."

He nodded. "Lot of time with nothing to do but think."

They went back to the couch. "I have a life, you know—friends, interests." She watched him and tilted her head as he reached for her windblown hair. His touch made her sigh. She closed her eyes and thought about him on the dike with the dogs at his heels and on the wharf with the wind. When his mouth covered hers, reality diffused into fragments of pleasure and a sense of comfort. For the moment he was wonderful to lean on.

"Why didn't you tell me right away about my mother? You've had so many chances," she whispered as his lips moved from hers.

"The chances have been yours, Holly. You could have put the pieces together long before this. And the risk that you'd tear back to Philadelphia or sign this over to the first developer had to be considered."

"Of course. You couldn't have an hysterical woman disturbing your sleep or your future, could you?"

"Easy," he said, fingers in her hair. "It isn't easy, though, is it? It's hell trying not to think about it, not to feel."

"What I feel for Peter Bancroft is easy. What you want me to feel for him is hell, Drew."

Drew brought her into his arms. "What I want is for you to find your own feelings. The rest will fall into place. Trust me tonight. This one perfect night, let me touch you. Touch me, just us... Don't be alone, not now."

She tried to choose words carefully, to push down the rush of her pulse. "What we've shared physically doesn't change anything else. It's just for the moment."

His hand skimmed the crepe of her dress until he cupped her breast. She was being smothered by her own response. Her head told her to pull away but she sat motionless, so acutely aware of his gentleness and strength that she almost ached for him.

His thumb moved to the tip, which hardened through the fabric until she put her head on the back of the couch and slowly arched her back. He moved to the other one, soft and pliant until the heat of his fingers made her sigh. There was no seduction, only certain recall of the moments already shared and a burning desire to retrace the steps.

Holly watched him. He tugged her wrist. "Not here," he whispered. When the house was dark and they stood beside the moonlit bed for the second time, he unbuttoned her dress and slid it off her shoulders. "I want you to remember this," he said, "the way I remember you, all the ways we're so perfect." He moved to slide the dress from her hips but she stopped him and reached for his tie.

She loosened it, opened the blue oxford cloth and slid her hands from his waist up over his shoulders. His shirt came off first and the feel of his rough hair on her palms and his muscles tight with anticipation made her knees weak. She sank onto the mattress as he eased the dress over her hips.

"I've looked at you so many times and thought of this. On the walk; while you listened to my brothers tonight; while you ate. There's nothing we can't get through when we're this close. You've barely scratched the surface… I want you to know what you can do and what you can feel. I want you free."

Her eyes widened in the gray light, the familiar gesture of her hand at her breast made Drew drop his gaze. Caution slowed her pulse but desire drove her on, desire to keep him ahead of her. She said his name and repeated it, enjoying the way it sounded and the way he responded as she unbuckled his belt. He stepped out of his pants and put her hands on the wide elastic of his shorts. Beneath the heel of each of her thumbs she could feel his hip bones. Drew's voice was husky, his breathing tight but he talked to her, urged her to continue, to explore, and while she did, he repeated every movement on her with strong, warm hands.

She arched and he slipped off the last of her underwear. She caught her breath. "Drew," she moaned, "this isn't like the last time."

He pulled the combs out and when her hair was a tangle on her shoulders he held her face, making her look at the desire in his. "No, it's more; it's deeper. You've gone further than you meant to because it feels better than hiding. I know you're not afraid of me, darling. Don't be afraid of yourself."

Her ears rang with her own pulse. She clung to him in the pillows as he put his mouth on the peaks of her breasts. "Let go of the past, Holly. Don't be afraid of it." Gently, her hands wove through his hair and pulled him closer. It stopped the torment of his words but increased tenfold the desire. She wanted to lie, to tell him this was nothing, when in fact it was everything.

Time fell away as she caressed him, massaged and built a hunger that stunned her. She was wrapped in his strength, permeated by their desire, overwhelmed by what poured from his heart. Drew lingered over every inch of her, until there was nothing in her but exquisite torment, not only for his body but because of her love for him. She opened her eyes and looked at the passion and urgency in his expression. In less than a breath she matched it and they soldered their need in a timeless rhythm.

"Love me, Holly. You can," Drew moaned as she moved with him. His physical demands shattered the barrier. "I do," she cried, "I love you." The weight of restraint was lifted and her heart opened like a flower.

There was a hesitation in the pattern; his chest expanded and against her breasts, his tongue traced the rim of her ear. He moved as if her words had unloosed the reservoir of hunger and strength he had held back. They were equals in their need for each other. There was no more control, no more talk. The friction peaked. She was engulfed by ecstasy as it spilled through Drew and swirled into her bones, then rushed with her pulse into every part of her that touched him.

Long moments passed as the intensity of the moment softened. He caressed the curve of her hip and kissed her hair as if he could slow the descent and hold back the inevitable.

Holly's sigh was deep and not from contentment.

"Hush," Drew said. "Your heart's still pounding. Lie in my arms for a while without denying everything you just felt."

"I'm not denying—I just want you to understand."

"Holly, it's all right to admit you love me. It's all right to admit you loved Peter."

"Love! You made me say it. Peter?" She searched for words. "I didn't even know him. My memories are those of a child and my present knowledge is coming from someone who is doing everything in his power to eradicate my common sense. After what I learned tonight, I can't believe you'd even bring it up."

Drew pulled the quilt over them. "Maria loved him."

Her voice knotted. "If you think having sex will make me lie here and discuss this, you're dead wrong."

He pressed his palm over her heart and opened his fingers on the rise of her breast. "There's so much fear in there you can't—or won't—recognize honest emotion when it cuts right through you. I just made love to you. You just made love to me, a pure clean emotion. You're scared to death of it because it binds you to this place and to those people."

"I'm not afraid of sex."

He lowered his voice. "I'm not talking about sex. I was there last night for the sex, city mouse. For the two-people-having-a-good-time. For you it was fun as long as your self-control was intact."

She turned from the moonlight. "I don't need you to lie there and analyze a few moments of enjoyment. I knew what I was doing. It was probably a mistake, but nevertheless, it was my choice. You're talking as though I were a virgin."

"Emotionally, you are." He smoothed her hair to soften his words. "Don't turn away until you can put the truth in perspective. All this time I've bent over backward to give you a sense of what is part of your life. I'm not trying to eradicate your common sense, Holly. Sometimes common sense makes no difference, anyway. God only knows where this will lead, but maybe it's time just to listen to your heart, for once.

Your mother and Peter were very much in love," he said.

"Then why didn't she marry him?"

Drew sighed and sat up against the headboard, his arm still around her. "I only know what Peter told me and it wasn't much. Way before your time, John Bancroft was in Korea and reported missing in action."

"I knew that. You're telling me that's when it happened?"

"They were two people fighting what they didn't even admit to each other until the crisis. Maria fell apart, I gather. Peter was there for her....Then later John was flown home. Things like this happen. They happen to good people, frightened people, men and women who never mean to hurt anyone, whose motives are love and caring. In this case it changed the course of Peter's life."

"Obviously my mother chose to stay married. A lot of people were hurt. It was a far, far better thing..." she finished sarcastically.

"I think they went through hell, all of them."

Holly listened to him continue the explanation and all the while she held back the question that opened like a black hole in the story. "But the affair ended with the war? My father came home and the three of them lived happily ever after, almost? Why did financial problems separate them ten years later when an affair hadn't? Peter and Maria must not have told my father about their affair." She came up on her knees in front of Drew and tried to read his face. She could see nothing but desire. "Why did Peter tell you all this?"

He put his hand on her stomach and smiled. "Because life has a way of maturing you if it doesn't chew you up. Peter was a survivor; he was a man who had enough tragedy in his life so that when he met it again in ours, after our parents were killed, he knew how to help us. He never gave in to pain and he saw to it that we didn't, either. Bittersweet Bogs grew out of that strength. It's not just a chunk of hills and sand and grass, Holly. For Peter it was a chance for a new life.''

"And the sale of it will be the same for me," Holly said.

Drew moved his hand absentmindedly to the underside of her breast where the softness brushed the back of his hand. She felt the touch of his knuckles and knew her nipple tightened. "I could have bet money you'd say something like that," he murmured. "Peter deserves your love. I'm going to leave in a minute and go back to my brothers so you can have your peace and quiet."

He kissed the softness his knuckles had brushed. "Lie here alone, darling, and think about it. Think about what tears men and women apart and what binds them together. I know endless stories about you, about your childhood, about Maria's descriptions in her letters, and they all come from the man who talked about you constantly because talking kept you alive for him, kept Maria alive.

"We hate what you're doing now but there isn't one of us who didn't love you. Peter saw to that."

Drew's words, capped by the constant caress turned the moonlit surface of her skin to gooseflesh. She put her hand on his wrist. "Drew, please. I have a whole life at home. I have friends, ambition, which doesn't include you and these churned-up memories. I may have said I loved you, I may have meant it, then. But once I get back, once this is all behind me, I'll forget. You'll forget," she finished weakly. "You have to."

She bit her lip and closed her eyes in an effort to control her feelings, but in the silence she caught the sound of Drew's quickened breathing. How had it happened, this complete knowledge of her desire? Why had she let herself pull him into her heart? She pushed his hand away but even the touch was superfluous; the arousal was complete in both of them.

The moment she opened her eyes, tears brimmed over her pupils. The hard planes of his body blurred until she blinked, but she didn't wipe them. Drew put his hands on her hips as she cupped the back of his head. "Heaven help me," she whispered against him. "I love you." The pattern of their breathing changed and they buried themselves in the rush. Just once more...this last time. Drew orchestrated the cadence they craved.

"Tell me you'll forget; tell me this isn't love," he said. They were perfect partners, replacing the wonder with certainty as rapture dissolved everything that separated them. The moment didn't pass, it grew to its crescendo, bound them in ecstasy and wrapped them in contentment. "Let me stay," Drew whispered finally, "Let me hold you all night."

Holly shook her head. "I can't. I need to think and you need to sleep. I already feel like I'm under a microscope."

The room grew cold as Drew dressed beside the bed. She lay still and watched the angles and planes as he moved. His hand tucked in his shirt, his fingers worked the buttons. Socks slid into polished loafers. When he finished he bent and kissed her.

"City mouse, this could last a lifetime," he said, smoothing the covers.

She trembled as she listened to him walk through the quiet house and close the door softly as he let himself out.

Eleven

The weather held. Outside the neat farmhouse the lawn was dusted with falling leaves. The plantings were trim, the orchard heavy with fruit. From the kitchen window, the bogs looked crimson even without a crop and the frame of pines added an oddly Christmasy touch.

Holly turned back to the photograph in her hand and looked once more at the black-and-white snapshot of Maria Bancroft as a bride with her arms around the brothers. The photograph joined the rest, and she left the folder on the table.

She made the call to Boston shortly after nine, then dusted the chair rail and wainscoting. She put birch logs in the fireplace and one last spray of berries and branches in a crock on the repaired hearth.

By the time the realtor and prospective client arrived, Holly was as neat and polished as what she was offering. In a blazer and wool slacks she went out to greet Jill Doucette.

"It's nice to meet you in person," the realtor said, introducing her to Mark DeLotta, the developer. "Isn't it everything I've told you?" she asked as they started along the perimeter. Jill looked at Holly. "I've been down twice since your attorney contacted us . . . A gorgeous piece with the rise and the view."

They started along the ridge as Jill gestured down the slope. "How charming! Cranberry farming right next door. You know they're all over the county."

"Harvesting," Holly said quietly. "The term is harvesting or picking. Cranberry growers, not farmers." She stood with them and watched the distant figure on the water reel as the reel churned through the bog, splinters of sunlight dancing off the water. Work had begun on the second set, and by afternoon the crop would be boomed and funneled up the elevator into the truck. Holly pressed her fist against the tightness in her chest.

"It's a family operation," Jill was saying. "The Flanigans grow for Ocean Spray. What a boon to their property value to have your design and construction up here."

"Branigan," Holly said.

The group turned back to the Bancroft side and skirted the orange markers. When they reached the neat row of apple trees, Holly took her fist from her ribs. "There's been a change. The bogs and the orchard aren't part of the package. Since they edge what I own, it shouldn't be a problem to shorten the parcel by subtracting this small piece of agricultural land. Kevin Branigan has made me an offer, one which would keep them in production . . .

It amounts to less than eight acres."

Mark shrugged. "No problem."

They wandered for an hour and finally approached the house. Once inside, she poured them coffee and accepted compliments on the antique detail. "Take your time and look around. There are three bedrooms and a bath upstairs in addition to the master bedroom and full bath down here." She watched Mark look at the fireplace wall.

Holly cleared her throat. "I had a chimney fire when I first arrived. In my haste to enjoy the atmosphere... I should have had it cleaned. Anyway, the repairs are done and I had a sweep give it a clean bill of health. All that remains is fresh paint or paper."

The developer ran his hand over the dentil molding. "Woodwork's in fine shape, sophisticated for so far out in the country. Maybe shipwright's touch? Horsehair and clamshell plaster, no doubt, probably built in the early 1800s."

Holly nodded, buoyed by his interest.

"We're always looking for detail like this for salvage."

"Salvage?" Alarm stabbed at her.

"Parts for new construction. I'd never raze something with this detail until we took the woodwork, moldings—" he turned and pointed "—raised panel doors, even the hardware if it's original. It would be part of my offer, of course."

Jill added enthusiastically, "It's amazing to watch. Mark could pry the whole mantel off without a splinter."

Mark nodded. "It's probably the best you could do since you're too far off the road to make moving the building financially viable. You look surprised."

Something twisted under her ribs. "I just didn't expect the house to be demolished."

"Of course. This is where the view is and if the bogs are to remain in production there are strict regulations about drainage and septic systems' distance," Mark continued.

Holly's smile was brittle. "Of course."

"If an offer is accepted, it's understood that you would receive design proposals and renderings," Jill said. "Although Mark's reputation speaks for itself."

They made small talk and when they reached the car, Holly shook both hands. "I look forward to hearing from you," she said firmly.

"Wonderful," Mark replied. "I'm sorry you seem upset about the house. Ones this old are full of sentiment, I know. You might consider holding on to the detail yourself. We could make arrangements, iron that out later. These old walls hold a lot of secrets."

She blanched. "The house means nothing to me, beyond its value as an antique."

Mark raised his eyebrows. "I misunderstood."

The subject changed to the weather, and after a round of handshakes again, Holly stood at the fork in the driveway and waved them off. She stayed a long time, running her toe through the peagravel and the realtor's visit through her head. She went back into the house and walked through the rooms. The second floor smelled musty; the bedrooms were sparsely furnished, barely used. In the bathroom the old footed tub had a worn spot in its enamel and the vintage toilet still flushed by the gravity-fed water closet at the ceiling.

Even though Drew had neatly removed and stored Peter's mementos, the charm and personality remained... Bancroft touches and Branigan before him.

Drew's grandmother had been a bride in this house; she'd raised her children here. Maria Bancroft had even seen this house, the year she knew would be her last. "Secrets, you bet," Holly muttered as she came down the stairs. Melancholy swept over her as she sank onto the bottom step. "Damn it! Damn all of you!" she cried with her head in her hands.

She imagined her mother in the orchard and Peter's explanation of why the trees had been planted. Where had Peter's strength come from to raise other people's children? Where did Maria's strength come from to make a marriage work . . . to travel such a distance after years of separation? It came from love.

For the first time since the truth had begun to unfold, Holly considered the possibility that it had been kept from her out of love. As a child, she couldn't possibly have understood adult pain but now as an adult it was time to come to terms with the aches of her childhood.

Holly got up, fighting the claustrophobic atmosphere. She felt selfish, like the woman the Branigans thought her to be, but as she looked from the parlor to the bedroom, anxiety tugged at her. She was scared of what she felt for Drew and the way it would cement her to this place. So much had transpired at Bittersweet Bogs and Holly had turned it all inside out.

She was close to tears as she went down the hill. Three of the brothers were working, all of them in waders. Ryan stood on the water reel, a lever in each hand as the submerged machinery churned. Holly concentrated on him rather than Drew and Kevin who were one bog over, wading through the berries on their way to the elevator.

She heard Kevin swear as he killed the engine that ran the conveyor belt up to the truck. The air was pungent with cranberries and traces of gasoline. Ryan nodded as she walked along the dike, but he kept on working. She had to force herself to keep walking.

Her anxiety deepened as she looked at Drew. She loved him. She wanted to run into his arms and think of nothing but their time together. Oh, God, how he could keep her from thinking.

"Company leave?" he asked when she was within earshot.

She nodded. "I promised you twenty-four hours, and I came down her to make sure you know that I'll keep my word." She watched him look at her. Color seeped across his cheeks; he took a deep breath. He's remembering, too, she thought, aching to touch his face. She shoved her hands into the patch pockets of her blazer.

Kevin looked up. "They make you an offer you can't refuse?"

She turned to him. "I've come to make you one. Is there a time when I wouldn't be interrupting?"

Kevin wiped his forehead with the back of his hand. "Not this week. Now's as good a time as any."

Holly took two deep breaths. "Assuming the developer makes me an offer, if things were to go through, I want to give you Peter's bogs and the orchard. No lease arrangement, just a title transfer."

Both men looked at her as Drew spoke. "You're talking about close to two hundred thousand dollars worth of property. Pretty hefty gift to soothe your guilt."

"It's not guilt" came too quickly. "The house, too, if you can move it or if you want the paneling and detail."

"Before they bulldoze it into splinters?" Drew said. "It sits—"

"I know damn well where it sits. You're suggesting that we move it down here for the next one of us who needs a house?"

Holly bit her lip and looked at the top of the elevator to keep tears from spilling. "I'm trying to be fair. It's just a possibility."

"Your timing's off," Kevin said. He glared at his brother.

"I'm sorry," she said. "I know I'm interrupting. Will you think it over?"

"About as much as you're tossing around our offer. If you'll excuse me, I've got problems even more pressing than you." Kevin turned back to the belt.

Holly backed up. "Of course." She looked again at Drew. "I don't suppose I could help?"

Drew gave her an incredulous look. "Leaving would probably be the best thing, Holly."

Kevin rolled back his flannel sleeves and worked his way out of the waders. He swore at the machinery; he swore at Drew, and after pulling workboots from the cab of the truck, he slammed the door and swore at them. She worked her way back over the dike while the brothers climbed onto the hood of the truck. Kevin went to the top of the elevator and Drew to the wooden rim of the flatbed sides, which held the beginning of the day's harvest.

She was miserable. Where was the solace in her generosity?

Kevin and Drew were arguing. Grown men using foul language to hide the pain. What did grown women do when they couldn't shut out the world?

"Tell her yourself," one of them said behind her.

"What's the point?" was the answer.

She stopped on the dike and turned back in time to see a blur of motion as Kevin lost his balance. His left leg plunged into the conveyor chain, belts and wooden lifts of the elevator. She screamed, "Drew!" as he reached for his brother from the rim of the truck box. Even over the putter of Ryan's reel, she heard the wood splinter. He grabbed Kevin's outstretched hand as the panel split beneath him. His foothold tore away, and in a motion that stayed with her for hours, the panel separated, spilling berries, wood and both brothers onto the ground twenty feet below.

Frantic, she followed Ryan as he jumped from the reel and plunged through the shin-deep water. He reached them just ahead of her, knelt and then got to his feet. "Don't let them move!" he barked. "I'll call the ambulance."

He yanked open the door of the cab and called the fire station on the truck's CB. Holly put her hand out to Kevin. His complexion had paled to alabaster and his grip nearly crushed her fingers but the blue language continued. He let go of her hand to reach for his ankle, but then, as if he had suddenly remembered, he turned to look at Drew. His younger brother brought himself up on one elbow and pulled matted cranberries from his hair.

"Be still, Drew," Holly said as he smiled drunkenly.

"Sure, babe," he whispered and slumped forward, an unconscious dead weight in the crook of her elbow. His head pressed her cheek and Holly knelt, immobilized by the fear that any movement would cause spinal injury. Ryan came back, reminded her that he was an emergency medical technician, and lowered his brother properly back down.

The distant wail of the ambulance siren drifted over the pines as Drew regained consciousness. By the time the vehicle had driven past the house and out the cart path, Drew was arguing with Ryan about his ability to sit up. It was not the first time Holly had felt invisible, but this time it was a relief.

"Stop acting like a damned cop and let me up!"

"Can it," Ryan said. "I'll make Holly sit on you."

"A pleasure," he groaned, "but I wouldn't be still."

Her blue eyes widened and the fear turned to embarrassment.

"Just my luck," Drew continued with a grimace, "to fall in love with a woman who gets me so rattled I can't keep my balance. Did she kill Kevin?" he asked.

The flush from her embarrassment paled. Beneath the joke lay the truth; they had been arguing over her.

Kevin closed his eyes. "I'm in too much pain to be dead," he said as the ambulance pulled alongside them.

Holly jumped to her feet, the first one to see Sean spring from the passenger seat. He looked down at his twin and then put his hand on Ryan's shoulder. "Keep Drew quiet. Kevin comes first."

Ryan shrugged. "Easy for you to say."

Over sarcasm and heavy language, Sean and his partner splinted Kevin's left leg. "I sure spend a lot of time saving people over here. Town's gonna start thinking it's nepotism."

Holly stood back. "I'm not related," she whispered.

Ryan heard. "You might as well be," he said.

When Kevin was secure, they applied a cervical collar to Drew. "I didn't land on my head," he complained to the sky as the medical technicians strapped both men to backboards. With Ryan's help, they shifted them onto stretchers. Drew was still swearing.

"There's a lady present," Ryan said finally.

"Whom I couldn't take my eyes off, which is how I got like this in the first place," Drew called as he and Kevin were put in the ambulance and the doors closed.

Sean locked the patients and technician in and looked at Ryan. "I suppose you and I get to clean this up."

"No doubt. Get going. Call me at the station. I'm working the desk."

"Drew seemed all right," Holly said weakly.

Ryan raised his head and looked at her with eyes like the twins'. "Let's hope so. Kevin's in bad shape. If it's a fracture they may put him in traction. He's gone for the rest of the season." He looked at his watch and then over her shoulder at the fire fighter's house. Holly turned to see what had caught his eye and watched Annie Branigan run from the field. She reached them breathless, her short red hair blown back from her face.

"What on earth—"

Ryan explained, omitting why they might have been careless.

"They fell!" She looked at the top of the elevator.

"And landed on solid Branigan backsides."

"They could have broken their necks!"

Holly shivered but Ryan smiled. "Drew waved a few fingers at me just to prove that he hadn't. Look, I've got to go get into my uniform. I'll stop at the hospital on the way to the station. Can you bring them home if they're released?"

Annie's face fell. "The kids are running fevers."

Holly touched her arm. "I'll stay with them."

Ryan made a hasty introduction, hardly necessary. "Let her," he added.

The stab of fear had passed, dulled into guilt, regret and a surge of affection for the man who teased her even strapped to a backboard. Holly looked at the new house. "They should be with family. You both go to the hospital; they need you. Anne, I'd be happy to stay with the children, really."

Forty minutes later, after more insistence, Holly sat in the quiet family room of Drew's twin brother. The children slept as emotions of every description surged through Holly, one trampling over the other. A tense situation had been made worse. *She'd* made it worse.

There were clouds over the late afternoon sun Holly watched through the windowpanes. The elevator stood abandoned; crimson-colored berries littered the ground. Above it all in the distance was the neat Bancroft farmhouse, the one that needed her touch.

At dusk headlights finally splashed along the side of the house, first Annie's station wagon, then Sean's small, red pickup. Holly was feeding ginger ale and toast to Kate while her sister watched *Sesame Street*. The parents entered together, and Holly answered the question before it was asked. "They were fine," she said. "A little surprised to see me but the tears didn't last long." She watched Sean scoop both of them into his arms and kiss their feverish little cheeks.

Anne smiled at Holly. "He's coming off a twenty-four-hour shift; you'd think he'd been gone a month."

Holly smiled, "How are Kevin and Drew?"

"Kevin has a compound fracture of the tibia, just above his ankle. They put him in a cast to his knee. They refused to release him until he promised to stay immobile for forty-eight hours. I told the doctor that two of his brothers are EMT's so they've sent him home. No movement except to the bathroom. He sounds like a wounded bear."

"And Drew?"

"No concussion. They put him in bed till the dizziness passed and they've told him twenty-four hours of rest, too. He feels like hell. He should soak the bruises."

Sean looked at his wife before talking to Holly. "We've got a crisis."

Holly looked from one face to the other and backed up. "You're not suggesting that I go take care of two wounded bears!"

Anne smiled. "My kids are sick, and Sean's just come off twenty-four hours of work. I'm sure Jody and Matt will come when they can, but, Holly, there's nobody else to get them through the night. Ryan won't be back till after midnight."

Holly sighed. "I suppose I owe them that much, but I can't imagine that Kevin'll let me in the door, let alone play nurse. Are there enough groceries for me to make them dinner?"

Anne nodded. "I'll bring some over tomorrow. I can put some casseroles together tonight, too."

The pit of Holly's stomach was tight. "Where are they now?"

"Propped in front of the wood stove, adjusting to the idea," Sean said.

"You discussed this?" Holly asked.

Sean grinned and looked exactly like his twin. "I wouldn't throw you to the bears without breaking it to them first."

The most difficult moment of all was the pause before she raised her hand to open the Branigans' kitchen door. Sean had driven her back to her house for clothes, then left her to the two dogs and two wounded grizzlies she expected to see on the couch.

Twelve

Her knuckles hit the outer door firmly, and without waiting she opened it and stepped inside. Her heart was in her throat, but she called, "Hello," as she put down the suitcase and entered the great room.

Max, Domino and Drew were on their feet. Drew was the one she expected to bark. Kevin was stretched out, still pale. A pair of crutches were propped against the wall. "Sean said you'd be expecting me," she said. "I'll make you some dinner and keep an eye on things until you can get straightened out...until you're feeling better."

"Better about what?" Kevin asked with his eyes closed.

Holly moved closer to him and put her hand on his shoulder. "I'm so sorry, Kevin, sorry about the accident. You helped me after the fire and I'm returning the favor. I can't make things right, but I can help." She looked at the dogs at her knees. "Sit, Max! Sit, Domino! You too, Andrew Branigan. You're to rest for twenty-four hours, too. Exhaustion is part of the reason you wound up like this. It made you careless."

"So did a wild-haired neighbor."

"Nevertheless, there's not a cranberry out there, spilled or floating, that can't wait. I'll take care of that myself, too, if I have to."

"I'd love to see it." He put his arm out for her.

"Sit down!" she cried.

"I didn't land on my head, kid, I landed on my—"

"Common sense. Now get off your feet before you land on it again. I came to make dinner, not argue sense into you."

Drew lowered himself into the chair. "No, talking sense has been my job, not that it's made a damned bit of difference."

There was a groan from the couch. "If I have to listen to any more of this, I'll send out for pizza and get rid of both of you. Knock it off!" Kevin pounded his pillow.

Holly blanched. "You're right," she said quietly. "I apologize. Leave things to me."

The men watched television news and weather while she searched through the kitchen cabinets, as foreign to her as her uncle's had been. The wind was still brisk, the sky overcast. It seemed one small favor that no frost was predicted.

She sautéed peas with onions and dressed up hamburgers with blue cheese and English muffins. Drew quipped that it was good enough for Santé as they ate off their laps, but even the simple meal was an ordeal for Kevin, whose appetite was dulled by the medication and pain. She got a glass of milk into both of them and drank a Molson ale from the bottle, which they found amusing.

Sean called for a progress report and added that both Jody and Matt would arrive the next day to put in as much time as they could. Matt was considering this his first house call, he added. She told the men and got them both to smile.

"Are you holding up all right?" Sean had asked.

"Yes. Kevin feels too lousy to scream at me. I'm having a tougher time with your twin, actually."

"Well, he's been hounding you right along. If anyone can handle him, you can."

Holly smiled in spite of herself. "I feel like Wendy with the Lost Boys or Snow White after she stumbled across the cottage."

She heard Sean take a breath. "Have you told them you're staying?"

"Me! I thought that was all arranged."

"I only got as far as dinner," Sean said.

Oh, God. "Then I'll stick to dinner. Ryan can take over when he gets off his shift."

"They won't cooperate for Ryan. Then he'll be up all night and Kevin'll wind up back in the hospital. They'll respond to you," Sean assured her.

"That remains to be seen." The gist of the conversation floated out to everyone in the room. Nevertheless, Holly asked that Sean tell Kevin, and she handed the phone over.

She watched Kevin listen; she watched Kevin look at her and she heard Kevin say, "You're out of your mind." He also mumbled in agreement and hung up.

Drew seemed cheerful. "Your choice of sleeping accommodations, darling. You can bunk with Ryan, share my bed or have Jody's room to yourself."

Holly bent to clear their plates and sniffed, "That doesn't even deserve a reply," as she took them into the kitchen. When the dishwasher had been loaded and the pans scoured, she went back to them and announced cheerfully that it was time to go up. Saying it made her heart jump.

"I'll stay down here," Kevin said.

Holly cleared her throat and pulled a piece of invisible lint from her pants. "Your room has a better view of the bogs. You can supervise from up there, read your frost monitor... It's next to the bathroom and I'll be across the hall."

"Wouldn't you know it," Drew added. "She's picked Jody's room."

Holly glared at him. "Will you give me a hand, Drew?"

Drew looked at his brother and got up stiffly. "The woman has a point, Kev. She's also extremely persuasive. Save your arguments for the big things."

"Thank you," Holly said to Drew. She put the vial of medication in her pocket, the crutches under Kevin's arms and eased him onto his good leg. The trip to the second floor was slow and painful. When they got to his room, Drew pulled back the spread and helped her ease his oldest brother onto the mattress. He left them while she put the vial on the bedside table and propped the pillows under his leg and behind his head.

"Give me a minute, will you?" Kevin asked.

"Of course," Holly murmured. "I'll come back when I've settled your brother." She went into the bathroom and turned on the faucets. While the tub filled she entered Drew's room cautiously.

He was stretched out on the fully made bed, one arm slung over his eyes. "Drew, I'm running a tub for you. A good hot soak will help the stiffness."

His free hand went out to her, and she took it as she sat on the edge of the bed. "You feel worse than you're letting on, don't you?" she asked.

"Physically? About as bad as you feel emotionally," he answered.

"That bad," she quipped.

Drew moved his arm away and looked at her. His green eyes were drawn at the edges, but the pupils were clear. "My bruises'll be gone in a day or two. How long will it take you to forget?"

Holly turned her head but he kept talking. "You won't forget. You can shove it somewhere behind those troubled eyes, city mouse, but you won't forget anymore than I will. Anymore than Peter forgot about Maria, anymore than Maria forgot about John."

"John? I thought the implication was that my mother never stopped loving *Peter*."

Drew pressed the puckered skin between his eyes. "What I know, I know from Peter. What was love for him was solace for Maria, comfort during a crisis."

Holly began to think, logically this time as she worked the pieces. "But I thought their affair lasted only while my father was lost in Korea," she cried. "Did it start again when the business was failing? Is that why he left? Is that why there was such a rift?"

"More or less," Drew hedged.

"And what makes you think this is any different, Drew? More than comfort or solace..." She didn't sound any more convincing than she felt. She felt like leaning over and wrapping her arms around him until they shut all the outside world away. Instead, she got up and told him the bath was ready and then went in and turned off the faucets.

Holly went back to Kevin's room as the bathroom door slammed. "Expressive," he said with a smile.

"That he is," she said, giving Kevin her attention. "The phone's within reach and your medication is, too. I'll get some water and a glass." She took a deep breath. "Now can I get you into some pajamas? You'll need help getting those jeans off. If you have some scissors, maybe I should cut the rest of them off so you don't have to move." She cursed the color in her cheeks.

"Seen one Branigan, you've seen them all, I guess."

Holly brushed at the air between them. "I think I like you better when you're furious with me."

"I'm still furious with you," he threw right back pleasantly.

"Well, anyway, I'm just a nurse at the moment. For heaven's sake, I've seen you in less than this the last time—after the fire. And there's nothing between Drew and me," she lied.

Kevin moved his head on the pillows. "You're too much like one of us to get away with that. You've got enough fight in you to stick to your scheme come hell or high water, but, Holly, you'd best take a good look around 'cause you and Drew are in high water right now, and it's still rising."

"Kevin, you need to rest. This conversation isn't doing you any good."

"It's going to play itself out one way or another, and there's hell ahead. I'll buy the song and dance about school tuition and a real career, but the bottom line is a vendetta against ghosts. You're swinging at Peter and the rest of your family and that affects mine. You were a very big part of Peter's life; you know that now. Drew doesn't deserve to have his heart torn out for helping you see that."

Holly looked at him, surprised at the concern. He wasn't talking about the sale of the Bancroft property, he was talking about her relationship with Drew.

"Drew seems quite able to take care of his heart," she said. Kevin was too uncomfortable to say much more, she knew, and before he had the chance she told him to rest while she got the scissors from Jody's room.

She took her suitcase with her, dropped her key chain in the ashtray and pocketbook on the bureau and found the sewing shears on the desk. Tomorrow, she told herself, she'd be back in Peter's house. Anything was bearable for one night.

She went back to Kevin as she heard the muffled sound of her name from the bathtub. "Holly? I need a hand getting out."

She put her face to the closed door. "A paw will have to do. You have your choice of Max or Domino. Pull a towel rack off the wall, if you have to."

"I thought you were here to nurse the injured."

Holly smiled to herself. "The injured party is in the next room. As a matter of fact, I'm about to get him out of his clothes..."

"The hell you are!" came next, followed by the *splat* of a washcloth hitting the door.

After one look at the pain in Kevin's face, she dropped the humor. "Let's get this done and get you to bed," she said gently and he didn't argue.

"I'll sleep in my T-shirt and shorts, if you'll just get me out of the jeans." He groaned as he moved. The left jean leg had been cut off at midthigh in order to set the cast. "Every inch of me is screaming."

Holly did her best to cradle him while he unbuttoned the corduroy shirt he'd worn all day. When that had come off he pulled off the undershirt. "There's a clean one in the top drawer."

Holly got it and sat gingerly, making sure she didn't disturb the cast. With slow, deliberate slices, she worked the scissors along his thigh, starting at the point where the emergency room doctor had stopped. She heard Drew come through the door and saw Kevin look at him.

"Eat your heart out," he said to Drew.

"My one consolation is that you're in too much pain to enjoy it," he answered.

Holly turned her head. Drew was wrapped in a towel, rubbing another over his hair. There was a cinch belt around his ribs. "Drew, you didn't tell me you broke your ribs!"

"Cracked a couple," he replied.

"Go back to your room and lie down!" Holly said over the final snip.

Drew came closer. "Not before *I* remove the jeans. Close your eyes, Holly."

"Juvenile," she muttered.

But Kevin added, "She says she's seen one Branigan, she's seen them all."

Even Drew blushed. "Holly said that, did she?"

"Of course I didn't," she protested, buoyed by the humor, cursing the warmth she felt them wrap her in. How extraordinary it must have been to grow up in this house.

Drew tugged the denim from under his brother while Kevin gripped Drew's arm. "God," he muttered through gritted teeth, "you've got the touch of a back-hoe. It's Holly or nobody from now on."

Drew turned and grinned at her. "Exactly how I feel."

She busied herself with the glass of water. "Put something on before that towel falls off."

Kevin relaxed as Drew went back to his room. Holly pulled the sheet over the cast and worked the blanket around it in an effort to avoid adding pressure. "Doze while I finish up downstairs. I'll leave a note for Ryan to stoke the stove, and after I let the dogs out I'll come back. You'll be due for more medication by then; that should help you sleep."

"I hope so," he added as she left the room.

Drew was on his bed, his wet hair still damp and disheveled. It softened his features and was all she dared look at before she touched the doorframe. "Put yourself to bed, Drew. I'll make breakfast whenever you wake up. Please try and sleep. You need it."

He pulled his knees up and shifted. "You know what I need."

She left them both, finished up downstairs and didn't return until the second floor was quiet. Both bedrooms were dark. Once in Jody's room, she pulled on her nightgown and let down her hair.

Such a short time ago they'd been anonymous. She sighed. There certainly wasn't anything anonymous about them now. She smiled to herself. After tonight she'd have spent time in three different beds in this house, fought with them all, baby-sat for one, undressed one and made love to one. "Made love," she whispered. "Oh, Drew, what have we done?"

She was relaxed, comfortable and sure that if she trotted down the hall, she'd find Drew with open arms. Whose heart was being torn out?

Shortly after midnight, muffled thuds below woke her up. She blinked, already alert, and didn't relax until she was sure it was Ryan stoking the stove. She heard him call the dogs and settle them before he climbed the stairs. She'd left a night-light on in the hall and her door open to listen for Kevin.

"Holly?" Ryan whispered.

She sat up, leaving her bedside lamp off but he came across the room like a man familiar with his surroundings, light or dark. It reminded her of Drew in Peter's house. "Thanks," he said. "We appreciate your staying." He touched her shoulder. "How are they?"

Her eyes adjusted to the low light; she could even make out his badge against the navy blue uniform. "Both asleep, which I take as a good sign. If they need anything, I'll get up. You sleep, Ryan. They're counting on you to finish up tomorrow. Your other brothers are coming home, too."

"I know," he replied. "I talked with Sean. Come get me if you need me." He laughed.

"What is it?" she asked.

He laughed again, hard. "This is a far cry from the conversation we had the first time I found you up here. I wish you could have seen yourself, grabbing those blankets with your hair stuck in the slats and the dogs..."

"Come on, Ryan. What did you expect! I thought you were Drew, which would have been bad enough, not to mention a police officer charging across the room at me." She sputtered and then laughed, as well. "Did you ever tell your friend Johanna about it?"

"No," he sighed. "We haven't spoken lately. Between my hours, the picking..." He moved back toward the door. "I guess it's been Drew's turn to get lucky."

Get lucky, she repeated to herself when he'd gone. They all referred to it, each of them holding back as if they knew she held the cards and couldn't quite believe she would stick to her intentions.

Down the hall she heard Kevin stir as his mattress squeaked under his weight. She lay still, alert, and didn't drop back off to sleep until she was sure he was quiet again. An hour later she was awake again. The light from the hall was brighter; Kevin had turned on his lamp.

Gathering her flannel nightgown, she tiptoed past Ryan's closed door and Drew's open one. Kevin was swearing, as usual, and a glass of water lay spilled. She went right to him. "I'll get it," she said as he looked up, propped awkwardly on one elbow.

From the bathroom she got washcloths to mop the spill and refilled the glass. As an afterthought, she took a fresh washcloth and wrung it out. Kevin sat up and tapped a capsule into his palm.

She handed him the glass, and when he swallowed the pill she took out the pillow, fluffed it and smoothed the sheet. Small beads of perspiration lined his upper lip. "Is it bearable? Ryan's home. We can take you back to the hospital."

He shook his head. "I'm okay."

She waited until he lowered himself back into the pillow and then wiped his forehead with the cloth. He growled and pushed her hand away. Holly looked at her watch. Fifteen minutes and the medication would take hold. She brought her hand back.

"Don't look a gift horse in the mouth, Mr. Branigan. I'm the only one foolish enough to get up with

someone as cranky and cantankerous as you." He
glared and she gave him her best smile. "Lie down. I'm
going to give you my best dose of mothering."

"Like hell," he said but it was punctuated with a
groan and he relaxed, keeping her hand away with a grip
on her wrist.

She stayed cheerful. "You know how stubborn I am.
Is it just your leg?"

"Mostly."

"Well, you sure don't take to being cared for any
better than I do. That comes from being on your own
so long and watching out for all these other crazy men."
He let go of her wrist, and she resumed wiping his face.
"Just think how many women would love to be in my
place."

"Dozens."

"You're modest. I know for a fact the country's di-
vided into fifths and there's a line from here to the Cape
Cod Canal for you. Drew told me." She lowered her
voice. "Is there anyone you'd like me to call tomorrow?"

"Word'll get out."

She smiled at his stern expression, watching for an
indication that the capsule was softening the hard lines.
His fist was not as tightly clenched. "I can't roll you
over, Kevin, but I can massage your shoulders from
here."

He gave her a half smile, and she worked the ridge of
his shoulders with her hands. In choppy sentences she
got him to talk about safe topics: his support of the
symphony, the harbor, hunting. She talked about her
love of Italian and her pupils, the foreign men and
women struggling to master English. There wasn't any

stab of regret for the loss of the job, however. It already felt simply like another chapter closed.

The medication was taking hold, and when she felt his hands relax she stopped and laughed softly.

"Funny?" he said groggily.

She smiled. "I was just thinking how shocked I'd have been if you'd told me a week ago that I'd be sitting on Kevin Branigan's bed in the middle of the night talking about life."

His eyelids were heavy, and her anxiety for him softened. "Or that you'd have fallen in love with his younger brother?" Holly didn't answer and Kevin continued. "Drew and his strays . . . first there were dogs and kittens and half-dead sea gulls. When puberty struck, half the town locked up their daughters. But I saw it in him the night we all sat down with you . . . your first night here. I think he went hunting the next morning to get away and try to figure what the hell hit him. I'm not sure he knows yet except that you're part of Peter, and in some crazy way that makes you part of everything he loves and admires."

Holly's eyes filled with tears, and she pressed her nightgown against them. "Kevin, I can't fall in love with Drew."

"But you already have. Pain isn't always physical."

Holly got off the bed and fussed with things on the bedside table. When she finally looked back, Kevin had closed his eyes. She smoothed the blanket and snapped off the light. The small night-light in the hall gave the illusion of candle glow, and as she stepped from the bedroom, Drew's distorted shadow moved along the hall wallpaper.

She gasped and touched her throat while her heart thundered. He was in his pajama bottoms, his chest cinched by the rib belt, leaning against his doorway.

"How long have you been out here?" she whispered harshly.

"Long enough to know that when you think no one's watching, the love for this family pours out of you like syrup."

She looked at the wallpaper. "Kevin spilled his water."

"You could have called Ryan. I know you wouldn't chance waking me up."

"I'm here so none of you has to be bothered." *Bothered*. She closed her eyes as the pounding worked its way into her temples. She opened her eyes as Drew's hands moved through her hair.

"I love you, Holly. I love the fight and I love the surrender...the way you look wrapped for frost and unwrapped for—" His voice caught and she took a step closer.

"Unwrapped for loving you, Drew," she finished. She put her face next to his and let her breasts mold to him. "What will I do?" she moaned as his arms tightened around her.

"I belong to all of this and so do you, Holly. It's in your blood as much as mine."

Her blood, at the moment, was beginning to simmer. When she pulled away, his lashes lowered, his eyes shadowed by a combination of desire and medication. "I think you've taken too many painkillers," she murmured, but when he smoothed the flannel over her breast and found the buds, she stepped forward.

"Nothing can touch the ache of wanting you," he said into the tangle of hair at her ear. "And nothing will make me believe that you don't see that it can work. You know it can. There's a place for you here where you can see accomplishment, where you can use that fire and fight to make things work . . . make *us* work."

"Here—"

He pressed warm fingers against her lips. "Don't cloud things by talking. Your answer is crystal clear, Holly. Your body doesn't lie."

Thirteen

She put her hands on his shoulders, drawn by what they had already shared. Joy bubbled inside as desire flared at every contact point between them.

There was enough power in Drew's kiss to make Holly believe in fairy tales. Maybe love would conquer all. They clung and caressed in the doorway as if the moment would never come again. Her body was alive with her need for Drew, for his strength and gentleness, for his wit and his warmth. The heartache, which always came with daylight, would be no worse for the joy he could give her now.

There were a hundred reasons why she should have pulled away and gone back to her room. There were two other men in the house; Drew was wrapped and sore. She felt him flinch. Emotion this deep, this encompassing, had no safety net. They caressed each other playfully at first until the give and take was no longer a game. Holly touched him as a woman finally sure of her need to express her love. Drew responded as though he sensed the change, as if it lifted concern and left nothing but his desire to return that love.

With a moan he pulled her into his room and closed the door.

"This must hurt," she whispered.

He smiled. "You have a way of making me forget."

Her heart thundered. "Are you sure?"

"I love you," he murmured, "and I've never been more sure of anything in my life."

Holly stopped talking. Drew didn't want her words, and she couldn't think of any; she couldn't think of anything except the joy she felt when she looked at him and her desire to express it.

Drew held her hand and moved to the bed, looking at her as though he could hardly believe she'd come with him. She could hardly believe it herself. It made her smile. "I'm really here," she whispered and untied the drawstring of his pajamas. "Try not to move too much. Let me help, Drew. I don't want to be responsible for any permanent injury."

His laugh was a throaty growl, and he eased himself onto his back. When he was comfortable, Holly stood beside him and pulled her nightgown over her head and then impulsively snapped on the light on the bedside table. Drew's smoky green eyes caught the glow, and she could see the lines of pain ease. "Holly—"

"Shh." She pressed her fingers to his lips and sat on the edge of the mattress.

She was aching for the familiar friction of his chest crushing hers, the rhythm of their bodies against each other. Instead she balanced carefully and, in one fluid movement, straddled him. Drew's hands flew to her hips as she kept her body pliant over him. His jaw clenched at the side of her face. "My God," he whispered, "you're full of surprises."

His grip strengthened her balance, and his hands brought her hunger to its peak. Like a whirlpool, it funneled into one central location as she watched his face distort, not with the pain she had feared, but the joy she had hoped for. The first tremor was immediate as she welcomed him. Drew's hands pressed her back, her bottom, her thighs as she shimmered. She moved her arms under his neck.

There was no holding back and in the quiet room, barely moving, she felt him tense. They muffled their cries and let their bodies speak as ecstasy thundered through them. Rapture was etched on Drew's face, and when Holly opened her eyes and read it in his features, contentment filled her. Love gripped her as the passion had.

She was satiated with it. She moved next to him as he kissed her eyes and her breasts. She kissed him back and lay molded to him until he fell asleep. Holly smiled; he looked none the worse for wear.

Leaving him was agony, tempered only by her realization that come first light, they had a whole future to discuss. She snapped off the lamp, dressed and left the door open in case he needed her. That thought made her grin. She went back to Jody's room and slept till seven.

The house was still quiet when Holly awoke. She pulled on jeans and a heavy sweater, piled her hair in the combs and tiptoed down the hall to check on her men. Outside Drew's open door, she brushed her fingers over the wallpaper where he'd cast his shadow. She bent and snapped off the night-light. Drew was under the covers, his peaceful face half-buried in the pillow. Love and concern knifed through her. He certainly didn't look the worse for wear; he looked gorgeous, even when he wasn't grinning that grin.

Kevin, too, was asleep, though the condition of his blankets told her it had been fitful. She left them and went down to make breakfast. She fussed over the food while all the emotions she'd been working so hard to deny filtered through her. Kevin had said she was in high water, still rising...

Still waters run deep, she thought in reply. All *they* needed was for her to take the property off the market and the waters would start receding. Loving Drew was a package deal, and she fried bacon wondering how many other crises she'd have ahead of her if she chose that future together. How many other decisions would come from Kevin, Ryan, Sean, Jody, Matt or Drew himself.

The coffee perked; she drained the bacon on paper towels and pulled frozen orange juice from the freezer. There was a ready-made pie shell on the shelf, and on a whim, Holly took it out, too.

A basket of her uncle's apples sat on the table and while the floor above her began to stir, she piled slices into the shell. At the sound of the back door, she turned to find Matthew Branigan. His arrival brought the dogs up from beside the wood stove, and after he let them out he greeted her warily.

Holly raised her peeler, trailing a loop of MacIntosh skin. "Hello," she said, self-conscious again. "I guess you heard I'm over here playing Snow White or Wendy or something."

Matt was pleasant. "My first chance to make a house call. Did you keep Kevin in bed?"

Holly nodded. "He had a bad night, but he did sleep. Drew'll be fine." She felt color rising through her complexion and turned back to the pie. "Tell Kevin I'll be up with his breakfast. The rest of you can eat here. I assume you all eat big meals in the morning when there's work ahead."

Matt looked over her shoulder and out the window at the waiting elevator and bog. "How'd they get so damned careless?"

Holly shrugged, biting back the urge to tell him she'd had a lot to do with it. After Matt had gone upstairs, she put the pie in the oven and glanced out over the view.

A life with Drew... The rest of them seemed to want nothing more than Bittersweet Bogs intact. She felt herself retreating. She could rent the property in Philadelphia; she didn't have to sell it... If things didn't work out with Drew. Things... together things? Forever things? Marriage? Partnership? Would they expect her to play Snow White if she wound up here? A relationship with Andrew Branigan was a package deal... She could apply to any number of schools in Boston for an M.B.A. program. There were possibilities...

Holly shook the stream of consciousness from her head and set a tray for Kevin. She walked through the house concentrating on the present. First things first, Bancroft. Let's worry about whether Ryan and Drew have their clothes on. Get through today; the M.B.A. can wait.

Kevin was holding court in his room, and from the animated sounds of all four brothers, Holly gathered that both he and Drew were feeling better. She shifted the tray and approached the doorway. Matt swore and looked at each of his older brothers. "And she still had the realtor here? Drew, you were so sure that once she came to terms with it, she'd change her mind! Ryan and Kevin, you've been here all this time; I can't believe you let things go this far. What the hell kind of chance is there now?''

Drew moved along the edge of the bed as Holly came into the room, but no one saw her. "Matt, I'm sure things will change. Hitting her over the head with everything at once would have driven her away. I thought she knew about Maria. Hell, she didn't even know about Peter having her photographs. She didn't even unpack over there, she was so uncomfortable.''

Holly froze, her face burning, but Drew kept talking. "She came all the way up here to unload memories of an uncle who turned his back on her. Vindictive? Maybe, but, Matt, I swear she didn't even know why.''

Ryan, Drew and Matt, all dressed, were on their feet arguing. It was Kevin, facing the door, who finally saw Holly. He put his arm up. "My breakfast's arrived,'' he said at the same time Matt added, "You're in love with her, every last one of you!''

"Matt!'' Kevin said again, and the room fell quiet.

The surprised stare of four silent men was as painful as their argument had been, but she was too far into the room to retreat. Instead, she swallowed, focused on Kevin's vial of capsules and walked to him. She lowered the tray. "There's a pie in the oven,'' she said, barely above a whisper. "After I change the linens in Jody's room, I'm leaving.''

Drew stepped forward and touched her arm. "Holly, wait.''

She shook her head. "When I came to Millbrook, it was to settle the estate. My reasons have no bearing on anything.'' Her voice caught and she looked at Drew.

"You've made everything so complicated... We have a lot to talk about, Drew, but unlike you, I have the decency to discuss my feelings privately. Right now I just want to get out of here, out of Millbrook. None of this means anything to me, not Bittersweet Bogs, not my uncle's relationship with you, or his with my mother," she lied. She had to blink hard, but there was no way on earth she would let herself cry in front of these men. "Peter Bancroft was nothing to me."

"Holly—" Matt said, but Drew raised his free hand and stopped his brother.

"Matt's right, city mouse, we all love you. No one more than I do, except maybe Peter Bancroft."

"He was nothing to me," she repeated, her voice quavering.

"He was your father," Drew said.

Holly stood rooted to the floor, unable to say *liar*. Unable to fight the army of emotion. She wasn't shocked, she realized. It was more a sense of relief that the final, crazy piece of the puzzle had been put into place. All she wanted now was to get out of this hated place, and at the moment she was willing to sacrifice whatever she might have had with Drew to do it. In a voice icy with calm she said, "I'm leaving."

They let her. Drew let go of her arm, and she left the room with reality at her heels. By the time she reached the hall, she had to steady herself with a hand on the wall. She entered Jody's room as the tears blurred her vision, and at the bureau she brushed furiously at her eyes. The ashtray was empty; her keys were gone. She was back in Kevin's room before any of them had left.

"Bastards!" she cried. "You've taken my keys." She pointed to Kevin. "You lectured me last night about the hell ahead, about Drew. Sean made me think I had to stay here and take care of you. You set me up, all of you! I want my keys. I want to get out of here!''

Drew reached for her but she backed up. ''I love you, Holly, enough to keep you from going through this by yourself.''

''What *you've* done is worse than the rest of them put together.''

Ryan moved suddenly on her right and scooped her into his arms. ''Let me down!'' she cried, outraged.

He grinned. ''Pretend I'm Drew. He can't play hero until his ribs heal.'' As she wriggled he walked out of the room and into his brother's. ''You might as well stop resisting. I subdue prisoners for a living. I'm not above handcuffing you to the bedpost to get you to listen.'' He put her on her feet and kissed her forehead. Drew sat on the unmade bed.

''Work your magic, Drew,'' Ryan said. ''Holly, I suggest you listen. There's nowhere to run except the bogs and if you go out there, God knows, we'll put you to work.'' Without another word, he left, closing the door behind him.

The numbness dissolved and she began to cry. Drew pulled her into his arms and down onto the covers. They lay that way a long time until his entire right side was warm from her and she was quiet.

''Holly,'' Drew whispered, ''it's important that you know that my brothers knew nothing of Peter's relationship to you until this week. When you made it clear that you were still going to sell, they wanted to hire an attorney and drag it through court; change the zoning, anything . . . I asked for time and told them why.''

''Things were so cut and dried. My life was in order, all of it.''

Drew shook his head at her words. "You don't believe that. You wouldn't feel this way if you did. Peter's will forced you to face childhood beliefs you'd carried for a lifetime. You've never understood why you felt so deserted. Vindication is a good word for what you're doing, Holly, but now you know the reason. Stay with me long enough to finish this once and for all." He chuckled softly. "The cop's got your keys, anyway, so you don't have much choice."

"Ryan thought of that? And sleeping with me—did you all toss a coin?"

Anger filtered into his hazel eyes, but it softened. "We haven't slept together."

"Well, you took me to bed."

"Say it, say it like you did last night," he coaxed.

"All right, *love*. We made love. Was that your idea?"

The smile grew sweet. "Making love was our idea, yours and mine, and the only thing we've agreed on since you came into my life. You fought that reality as hard as you've fought the truth about Peter. Holly, darling, I've loved the idea of you since my hormones started working. I used to fantasize about the niece in Philadelphia coming up for a summer...But you in the flesh—" he paused to make sure she was fighting a reluctant smile "—I've never seen such strength. I've never known such gentleness, such love. Don't you see what Peter's done?"

"Turned me inside out, thank you very much."

"He's brought you home."

Holly moved her palm over his chest, over the Christmas red flannel shirt and the rib belt. Somewhere beneath it all a heart beat strong and steadily, one with room for her in it. Her head filled with questions. "How long have you known?" she asked softly.

"Since the time your mother came to visit. A long time ago Peter fell in love with his brother's wife. It was platonic and a comfort for both when John went to Korea. They were family, but when John was reported missing it was a trauma Peter and Maria faced together. It brought them closer—too close."

Holly's laugh was hollow. "Especially when they found out about me."

Drew immediately wound her fingers through his. "You know your mother's medical history. Pregnancy was thought to be nearly impossible. Peter told me it complicated her problems and she wound up having a hysterectomy after you were born. Even so, no one thought of you as anything but a miracle."

Holly's heart jumped. "My father—John—didn't know, though, did he? The timing must have been so close to his return from Korea that no one suspected." She put her head in her hands.

"No one suspected," Drew repeated. "And you were Maria's only child. Peter didn't ruin the business partnership, Holly. It failed—that much is true and in that crisis Peter turned, again, to Maria...two people fighting to keep the kind of bond you and I have. This time John found out and put the pieces together... three lives shaken, changed forever but there was enough compassion in all of them to spare the one person they loved equally. You were ten and they told you Peter had to go. They blamed it on the business. It was to ease the pain of a child.

"I want you to understand, Holly, that divorce was out of the question. Peter wanted it; Maria refused. She had a life with his brother and she stayed maybe for your sake, too. John made it clear he wouldn't give her custody if she left, so Peter did. The money, no matter what John told you, came from their combined savings and got Peter started. It guaranteed that he would be out of their lives. He was a passionate man with a lot of empathy. He considered it an act of providence that so soon after he settled here, the six kids of the man he'd worked for were left without parents. He said it gave him the reason he needed to keep living."

"And he never saw my mother again except the one visit?"

Drew nodded. "That one time. She wrote, sent pictures of his daughter and came to Millbrook when she knew she was dying. When she'd gone back to Pennsylvania, I found him in the orchard. I was about twenty-two by then. He'd kept all of it to himself for eight years, but her visit was too much. He told me everything that afternoon. After that it was a bond just the two of us shared until this week. I thought for a long time I loved you because of Peter, but it's more than that."

Holly wiped her eyes, sure they must be puffy and bloodshot. "I have a pie in the oven," she said, but she made no move to get up.

Drew laughed. "I'm getting too close again. You absorb all this first. I have more files when you're ready. I have your mother's letters and a letter from Peter that I couldn't let you see until you knew."

"For me?"

"Yes. A letter telling you that this land is yours, that it's now part of you through Peter the way it was part of us through my grandparents. He made no stipulations, but it was his dying wish that I make you understand that you've had the best life, the most secure one three loving people could give you. He knew you were lonely but he also knew you were self-sufficient. Look at the turmoil you're in now. He would never have done this to you when you were younger. Peter knew I'd never let you go through this alone.''

He sighed and lifted her face. "If it's school you want so badly, we'll find a way to float another tuition. Don't sell this just for an M.B.A. If you want to give us the bogs and the orchards, the least we can do is make you Ivy League with the profits.''

Holly cried and then laughed and finally choked on hiccups. "Peter Bancroft knew perfectly well that if I came up here my life would turn upside down. He probably knew, he probably banked on the hunch that I'd fall in love with one of you.'' She wagged a finger at him. "Not even just one of you, Drew, you poor thing. He worked on *you* all his life; he set us up, you and me. What would he have done if you and I married other people years ago?''

Drew was grinning. "He would have rested a lot easier.''

"Why didn't you?''

"The girl next door, apple pie, everything. What more could I want?'' Drew answered.

Holly sat up and looked down at him. What more could *I* want, she thought. Out loud she sighed. "Andrew Branigan; it's a good name. You've met tragedy head-on and you've survived. Oh, Drew, there's so much you can teach me. There's so much I could learn here.''

She bent over and kissed him, letting her hair fall against his temple. "I love the way you touch my hair. I love the way you kiss, too, and your body, well...''

Color was creeping up from his open collar. "There's something about a man who blushes that knocks my socks off. Your love pours out of you like syrup. You wouldn't have said it about me, Drew, if you hadn't recognized it in yourself." Her voice broke and he caught her fingers. She pulled them to her cheek.

"To give so freely, so deeply, comes from being loved that much. Drew, that comes from your parents and from Peter who must have seen to it that none of you became bitter."

"In time you'll see that he did the same for you, in his own way," Drew replied.

Holly nodded. "I need you, Drew. I tried so hard not to, but I need your strength to help understand this. I think it's time I unpacked my suitcase."

"I love you, Holly," he said, moving his fingers into her hair.

"I'm glad," she said, "because I have to call the realtor and let them know Bittersweet Bogs is off the market. I have to wangle my keys back from Ryan and make sure Jody arrives. I have to make dinner for all of you starving cranberry growers and I should offer to help harvest. I have to make sure Matt can keep an eye on Kevin and that he's resting, and after all that I'll need a man who's so besotted with love that he won't notice I'm worn to a frazzle."

Drew laughed, and it touched all the places that ached for him. "I love you," she added. "I need you to help me remember and I need you to help me forget." She bent again to his ear, feeling his arms tighten around her. "After all the rest of you are taken care of, fed and tucked in, we'll go back up the hill, Drew, and you can keep your promise to Kevin."

"My pleasure," he whispered. "I'll see to it that you don't disturb his sleep. In fact, late tonight when you're in my arms might be the right time to consider making it a permanent arrangement."

ATTRACTIVE, SPACE SAVING BOOK RACK

Display your most prized novels on this handsome and sturdy book rack. The hand-rubbed walnut finish will blend into your library decor with quiet elegance, providing a practical organizer for your favorite hard-or soft-covered books.

Only
$9.95

**Approximately
16" x 8"
when assembled**

Assembles in seconds!

To order, rush your name, address and zip code, along with a check or money order for $10.70 ($9.95 plus 75¢ postage and handling) (New York residents add appropriate sales tax),payable to *Silhouette Reader Service* to:

In the U.S.

Silhouette Reader Service
Book Rack Offer
901 Fuhrmann Blvd.
P.O. Box 1325
Buffalo, NY 14269-1325

Offer not available in Canada.

BKR-2

Silhouette Brings You:

Silhouette Christmas Stories

Four delightful, romantic stories celebrating the holiday season, written by four of your favorite Silhouette authors.

Nora Roberts—*Home for Christmas*
Debbie Macomber—*Let It Snow*
Tracy Sinclair—*Under the Mistletoe*
Maura Seger—*Starbright*

Each of these great authors has combined the wonder of falling in love with the magic of Christmas to bring you four unforgettable stories to touch your heart.

Indulge yourself during the holiday season . . . or give this book to a special friend for a heartwarming Christmas gift.

Available November 1986

Silhouette Desire

FOUR UNIQUE SERIES
FOR EVERY WOMAN YOU ARE . . .

Silhouette Romance

Heartwarming romances that will make you laugh and cry as they bring you all the wonder and magic of falling in love.

6 titles per month

Silhouette Special Edition

Expanded romances written with emotion and heightened romantic tension to ensure powerful stories. A rare blend of passion and dramatic realism.

6 titles per month

Silhouette Desire

Believable, sensuous, compelling—and above all, romantic—these stories deliver the promise of love, the guarantee of satisfaction.

6 titles per month

Silhouette Intimate Moments

Love stories that entice; longer, more sensuous romances filled with adventure, suspense, glamour and melodrama.

4 titles per month

Silhouette Romances
not available in retail outlets in Canada